One More Time

BOOKS BY FAITH BALDWIN

Three Women
Departing Wings
Alimony
Office Wife
The Incredible Year
Make Believe
Today's Virtue
Skyscraper
Week-End Marriage
District Nurse
Self-Made Woman
Beauty
White Collar Girl
Love's a Puzzle
Innocent Bystander
Wife Versus Secretary
Within a Year
Honor Bound
American Family
The Puritan Strain
The Moon's Our Home
Private Duty
The Girls of Divine Corners
Men Are Such Fools!
That Man Is Mine
The Heart Has Wings
Twenty-Four Hours a Day
Manhattan Nights
Enchanted Oasis
Rich Girl, Poor Girl
Hotel Hostess
The High Road
Career By Proxy
White Magic
Station Wagon Set
Rehearsal for Love
"Something Special"
Letty and the Law
Medical Center
And New Stars Burn
Temporary Address: Reno

The Heart Remembers
Blue Horizons
Breath of Life
Five Women in Three Novels
Rest of My Life with You
Washington, U. S. A.
You Can't Escape
He Married a Doctor
Change of Heart
Arizona Star
A Job for Jenny
No Private Heaven
Woman on Her Way
Sleeping Beauty
Give Love the Air
Marry for Money
They Who Love
The Golden Shoestring
Look Out for Liza
The Whole Armor
The Juniper Tree
Face Toward the Spring
Three Faces of Love
Many Windows
Blaze of Sunlight
Testament of Trust
The West Wind
Harvest of Hope
The Lonely Man
Living By Faith
There Is a Season
Evening Star
The Velvet Hammer
Take What You Want
Any Village
One More Time

POETRY

Sign Posts
Widow's Walk

One More Time

BY FAITH BALDWIN

❦ ❦ ❦ ❦

HOLT, RINEHART AND WINSTON

New York

Chicago

San Francisco

F

Published simultaneously in Canada by Holt, Rinehart
and Winston of Canada, Limited.

ISBN: 0–03–091385–3

Library of Congress Catalog Card Number: 78–182770

Designer: Mary M. Ahern

Printed in the United States of America

Grateful acknowledgment is made to New Directions Publishing
Corporation for permission to reprint a brief excerpt from
Summer and Smoke by Tennessee Williams.

FIRST EDITION

ACKNOWLEDGMENTS

As EVERYBODY got into the act, this book is dedicated to many (otherwise blameless) people: to Doctor Donald E. Tinkess, long my friend, who took me to Doctor Edwin H. Kent, who restored my sight (and twice introduced me to a disembodied voice named Doctor Campbell)—and to my special nurses, who were just that . . . particularly Alice H. Wilson, R.N. (who went the second mile), and my old friend, Elizabeth D. Tocci, who listened to me complain nights, and who, when I came home, officiated in various capacities.

There were others, patient with the patient. Gratitude is due my longtime companions, Claire A. Lycett, R.N., and Shirley R. Ayers, R.N., friends and neighbors on and off duty. I am deeply indebted to Constance Taber Colby (for taking me to college) and to Elizabeth Young (for showing me Spain); to my daughter, Ann Cuthrell; my sister, Esther Bromley; and my friend, Walter J. Shaw. They'll know why.

Also, to a comrade of over twenty years, Agnes DuBay, to other friends and relatives, and to various wireless stations (one, especially) which kept me from climbing walls, a practice frowned upon by hospital authorities and not encouraged at home.

Thanks, Gang!

"Men tire of wars, of killing and being killed.
Empires rise and fall. It will always be so.
And in the eyes of Allah, each generation, with
its differences and similarities, represents,
simply, one more time . . . *la illah illa allah*."

*From the private papers of a
Turkish gentleman, born
c. 1454*

One More Time

1

CYNTHIA PEMBERTON WARREN stood by her bedroom windows and watched Edward, her husband, drive off with a scattering of gravel and a snarling of brakes, his destinations being his office in an advertising firm and his university's club, both in New York City. The month was June; the dazzling day, a Friday. Young leaves were crowding on branches trimmed with vocal birds.

Cynthia was a fortunate woman, endowed with good looks—all the Pembertons were handsome—excellent health, and a trust fund conservatively invested. She had two teen-age daughters who so far had given her only slight and normal cause for anxiety, and an attractive husband who had fathered them. In addition, he'd given her this big substantial house with its two well-kept acres, a swimming pool, a four-car garage and workshop with living quarters for the chauffeur or couple they didn't have, or need. Despite wars, rumors of more wars, unemployment, and an undeniable recession, Ed Warren could still give her Europe, Asia, and Caribbean cruises, not to mention minor amenities such as a well-stocked wine cellar, and, in this spacious bedroom, a walk-in closet with built-in sachet-lined lingerie drawers, slanting shoe shelves, sweater and handbag shelves, plus accommodation for innumerable garments hanging in neat aromatic splendor.

Cynthia walked away from the windows, paused beside a small, antique table, and picked up, as if absentmindedly, its sole ornament, a T'ang horse (guaranteed genuine on their last quick trip to Hong Kong), and flung it hard and straight-armed at the nearest wall, against which it shattered.

The birds went on singing, a timid breeze ventured in from the beautiful, polluted Sound, and Mrs. Warren cast herself upon a chaise and exploded into tears.

The record player down the hall stopped; there were light running footsteps; the bedroom door bounced open and "What happened?" asked Viki, her nineteen-year-old, briefly home from college.

"Nothing. Go away," said her mother, her face and lashes wet, her red hair disheveled.

Viki sat down on the end of the chaise and touched the maternal hand. "Hey," she said, "let it all hang out. . . . No, wait a minute." She rose, a tall slender girl with hair the color of an Irish setter's coat, walked across the room and quietly closed the door. Coming back, she took a handkerchief from the pocket of her masculine shirt. "It's clean," she remarked, with some astonishment. "Here, take it." She stalked into the bathroom—an elaborate affair, gold, white and pink, more Hers than His—returned with a facecloth and a hand towel, and briskly mopped her mother's face and dried the tears.

"Which tranquilizers are you using?" she inquired.

"Never mind. I don't need a tranquilizer," Cynthia said, trying to keep her breath from catching. "I'm all right. I dropped the T'ang and I'm fond of it." The tears began again, less violently.

"Probably came from across the border originally," Viki

remarked. "I never liked it." She vanished into the bathroom again and emerged with a glass of water and a tablet. "This ought to do," she said.

Her mother ignored her. "Where's Jenny?" she asked.

"She went riding after breakfast with Florence Owen."

"She didn't tell me——"

"Oh yes she did—at the table. You didn't listen."

"But she can't stand Florence!"

Viki explained carefully, "They're neighbors and class-mates. The Owens have horses; Jenny's on a horse kick just now. Also, Florence has an older brother and Jenny's seven-teen—graduated with honors from Country Day and going on to college—remember?"

"Where's Mrs. Larsen?"

"She and Edna are enjoying a cup of coffee in the kitchen. They couldn't have heard the crash."

"Edna can sweep up," said Cynthia vaguely, "when she comes to do the rooms." She sat up straight, and again, as if absently, reached out, this time taking the water and the tablet from the table by the chaise.

"That's better," said Viki. "Forget the lousy T'ang. . . . You and Dad took to hand-to-hand combat last night. I had the radio on and turned it up, but I heard." She added with unusual gentleness, "What's the matter, Baby?"

"Your father has left us," Cynthia said bluntly, and the tears stopped.

"You, perhaps—not us." Viki moved from the chaise, eased herself into a chair, her long legs under her. "Well, it's been nine years since the first time. . . ."

"You remember?"

"Of course. I was nine. . . . He'll come back, Mom."

"He needn't bother," Cynthia said acidly. "I'm fed up." She looked across at Viki. "Sorry," she added with an effort.

"For what? For telling me—or that you've had it? Nuts to the generation gap along with the Chinese horse. I'm involved in this; so's Jenny."

"Don't say anything to Jenny!"

"Why not? Dad won't be coming home—for a while anyway—and there isn't much business now on the West Coast. What excuses are you going to make?"

Cynthia said after a moment, "You're very callous, Viki."

"Tell that to——" Viki stopped and smiled; she had an enchanting smile and, at the corner of her generous mouth, painted a glistening non-color, a small dimple. "I was about to make a joke in very bad taste," she said. "I'm not callous. I'm a realist. . . . Who is it, this time?"

"Who is what?"

"I'm asking you," Viki reminded her, with admirable patience. "Girl, woman—or whatever? Nine years ago it was the brunette in the office."

Cynthia said with considerable dignity, "I can't discuss this with you."

"Why not?"

"You have no feeling for me, nor are you aware that your father and I are not compatible——"

Viki snorted slightly. "Come off it, Mom," she advised. "Of course I have feeling, as you put it, and I've grown up with other kids of non-compatible parents. When I was a kid, I used to envy some of them . . . all those bribes. I haven't lived to be nineteen without observing that Dad, as long as I can remember, has strayed a little—or a lot. I dunno whose fault it is."

"Whose fault!"

"Mac always says it takes two . . ." her daughter suggested." Her brown eyes, very like her father's, flickered away.

"Mac?" asked Cynthia, bewildered.

"My young man, Paul McDonald. You met him; he came out to Westchester last Christmas."

Viki got to her moccasined feet, and tossed back her mane of hair. "I hear Edna," she said. "Better be busy about something. I don't know if Jenny will be back for lunch or not. I'll tell Mrs. Larsen that the Mister won't be home for dinner. She'll think it's because he hates the Friday cleaning-team day. Mrs. Larsen does too, so Friday dinners aren't gourmet."

Her mother said suddenly, "Tell Mrs. Larsen I'd like early lunch, please. I'm going to call your grandmother and drive up for the weekend."

"May I go? I don't know if Jenny's planned anything or not."

Her mother said doubtfully, "I don't like to leave you girls alone, of course, but——"

"As to that, Mrs. Larsen rides a mean shotgun, and I wouldn't be alone for long. I'd like to see Gran. I promise I'll leave you alone for as long as it takes to tell her."

"I've no intention of telling her."

"I'll take my car," said Viki, "and poke round the countryside"—she paused at the door— "that is if you're sure you're all right to drive alone."

"Don't be silly," said her mother crossly.

Viki went down the hall to her room, which was her mother's and Edna's despair. Posters and blowups of the currently in, usually deceased, motion-picture stars. Books, records, the radio, the stereo, the small TV set, the sarape on the bed. Her room at Blue Mountain College was like it, although more so, as she shared it with Linda Foster. She thought: So I'm silly, but for my money, Mom's stupid.

Later, going down to the kitchen, she reflected: It's difficult enough to learn something about yourself without trying to understand other people—even Mac. She thought of her mother as a smooth, usually unruffled image . . . not that she couldn't be ruffled, but Viki hadn't caught her ruffling often. She thought of her as an expensive scent and a pleasant voice, which could grow sharp. She thought of her as someone with whom she was biologically involved simply because see was her child; and as a presence, often rebuking, but an admirable person in her own way. She didn't get bombed; she didn't meet Mr. Whosis over on Colony Road at a motel in another state; she didn't do many of the things other mothers did. She was a splendid hostess, and had time for her husband and children—or had, once. Now, thought Viki, I don't suppose we have the time for her.

Entering the kitchen, she agreed with herself that for no clear-cut reason she loved her mother and was sorry for her. . . . And the same goes for my old man, she concluded.

What a mess almost everyone made of their lives and other people's—adults, kids, or countries for that matter. She'd said as much to Mac once, and he had replied that it had probably always been that way; people making a mess of things and some of them getting it straightened out eventually.

Mrs. Larsen was patently relieved when informed that probably no one would be home for dinner or the weekend. "Father will be away on business. Mother and I may go to Mrs. Pemberton's—Mother's calling her now," Viki said.

"And Jennifer?" asked Mrs. Larsen. She had been with the Warrens for some years. She made out the menus, following Cynthia's suggestions; dominated tradespeople; terrified Edna; kept a watchful eye on Fred, the gardener, and an occasional helper; and intimidated the weekly cleaning team. Contrary to accepted notions, she was not fond of her employers except vaguely, Jenny who was still, in her opinion, a child one could scold. Viki had become alien to Mrs. Larsen when she went off to college. Edward and Cynthia she

8

tolerated; of the two, she liked Edward the better, but respected Cynthia.

Mrs. Larsen was a childless widow and, having worked in a number of big houses, knew better than to become attached. An energetic, efficient woman, her chief devotion was to whatever job she happened to have. She had no hang-ups and no affections, except for her cat and for a worthless nephew whom she saw occasionally, here or on her days off. She and Edna had bright comfortable quarters over the kitchen, which was big, modern and full of her own flowering plants. This part of the house was hers, and she rather resented her days off—every other Sunday after breakfast; every Thursday after lunch.

As Edna lived in the Village, Mrs. Larsen allowed her several evenings off during the week and an occasional Saturday. Now and then she condescended to blow Edna to a movie, which was usually rated R. She disapproved, but considered it her duty to warn, instruct, and admonish the younger woman. Mrs. Larsen never doubted that Edna was stupid—in which she was right; the good, obedient daughter of an elderly decent couple. Well, she was obedient to an extent, but knowledgeable beyond Mrs. Larsen's wildest dreams.

The late Mr. Larsen had been a robust beer-loving gentleman, who had worked now and again. In those days his wife had gone out to serve or cater, by day or evening. Her brief marriage had been sufficient for her and when he died, due to falling off a ladder, she wore black and was relieved. Her reading was mainly movie and TV magazines. The changing world had never much disturbed her, except economically —she remembered the thirties—and now many people were again cutting down, or even doing without, domestic help. She knew a lot of the domestic employees in this area. None, she considered, had as good a position as her own and she intended to keep it, even if her salary had to be cut. She listened to backstairs gossip with great interest, but knew enough to keep her own mouth shut.

Jenny's dog, Maisie, came to bark at the back door, an amiable cocker spaniel which Mrs. Larsen tolerated. Her own personal pet was a big white cat, Frosty, who got along pretty well with Maisie.

Viki said, "As soon as I know about the weekend, I'll tell you. . . . Mother would like early lunch, Mrs. Larsen. I'll try to get hold of Jenny." She went out, and Maisie followed her.

Mrs. Larsen sat down to make supply lists; one, if only Jenny were to be home tomorrow; another if Viki, her mother, and Mr. Warren were, and still another if she and Edna were to be alone. She thought about Viki . . . her clothes, such as they were; her wild hair, loose or in pigtails. Mrs. Larsen was glad she hadn't a daughter to raise or for that matter a son, judging by the young men who came to this house, or whom she saw around town.

Viki went back to her room which, as yet, Edna had not touched, so she went down the hall, knocked at Cynthia's door and entered immediately. Edna was tidying up the bathroom; Cynthia was packing a bag. "You called Gran?" Viki asked.

"Yes, she expects us before dinner. What about Jenny?"

"She hasn't turned up. I'll call the Owens' in a few minutes. If she's not there, I'll leave a message."

Cynthia, now her seemingly unflappable self, looking elegant in a navy pants suit, said, "I hope you'll take something besides those shorts to your grandmother's."

"Gran digs shorts," said Viki, "but—well—sure, jeans, boots, sweaters——"

10

"Do you never wear a dress?"

"Now and then, long and elegant, short and provocative, or sort of floppy-granny."

There was a clatter on the stairs and Jenny came bouncing in, out of breath as usual. Jenny, very like her mother, was fair and blue-eyed and for much of the year, tanned. She was not as tall as her mother or sister, and until this year her father had called her "Twiggy Jr." But now Jenny had acquired a neat little shape, currently unconcealed in a tight shirt and blue jeans, cut off at the knees and also tight.

"Terrific ride," she said. "Where's Maisie?"

"In my room. . . . Did Bo ride with you?"

Bo was John Owens, Florence's brother.

"Natch. I wish Dad would buy me Flash. That horse is something else and Florence says her father wants to sell him."

"Your father can't buy you a horse," said her mother. "There's a recession—or didn't you know it?"

"One year from this August," said Jenny, "I'll have my own income, thanks to Granpop. Might run to a horse. . . . You girls going somewhere?"

Edna, scurrying from the bathroom with her usual Larsen-induced timidity, disappeared. And Cynthia said, "Viki and I are going to your grandmother's for the weekend. Do you want to go—in Viki's car? I'll take mine."

"Gosh, I'd like to," Jenny said astride a chair, "but I told Florence I'd ask you if I could spend the weekend with her. Bo's having some guys down from school, and there'll be a rock session and all that jazz. Give Gran my love. I hope I get up there this summer." She added that she'd be busy. Her Country Day School had gone all out for Ecology and she was on the permanent Clean-up Committee; and "I'm going to get some sort of a job, maybe. Volunteer."

"Commendable," agreed her mother. "Does it ever

11

occur to you to clean up yourself? And are you lunching with us, or the Owens?"

"I'll give you that pleasure," said Jenny. "Then I have to throw a few things in a bag. I'll walk over to Florence's or Fred can take me in the truck."

She went out with Viki. Edna was buzzing about with the vacuum. Later she would dust with care, but she knew better than to disturb the stacks of records in each girl's room.

"I'm going to use the phone," said Viki. Between her room and Jenny's there was a small sitting room, where they had their own shared telephone.

"Calling Mac?"

"Yes."

"Wow," remarked Jenny. "May I listen?"

"Don't you always?"

Jenny sighed. "Sure; not that it does me any good." She stood in the sitting room full of their differing belongings and scratched her back against the edge of the open door. "I can't wait till I get to Blue Mountain."

"You won't have too long."

"September. Smashing. If I have as much fun as you and Linda."

"I've told you a thousand times that most of the students at Blue Mountain know that if they're ever going to get anywhere they have to work. And as a freshman you'll have to live in special dorms; you've been there; you've seen them. And you'll have to bring a letter from the Aged Parents, stating their position on weekend trips away from school. Even if you get unlimited freedom—I had to struggle for it—the Dean must approve, and you sign a pledge to honor parental rules."

"Boring," Jenny decided, "but there's got to be some excitement. Like the strikes and sit-ins in your freshman year."

"Oh, I went along with all that for a while— until I

12

discovered I was simply conforming. I had no actual passion to make the scene. Anyway, Blue Mountain's singularly free from all that. There are student activities, which you might like; the choir for instance. You have a good voice."

Viki shut the hall door and picked up the telephone. Mac was briefly with his family on the Cape. She looked at the scrawled telephone number under the instrument. And dialed.

After a short exchange of question and answer with someone on the other end of the line, Viki said, "Hi, Mac. . . . Yes, I'm home, but my mother and I are leaving after lunch for my grandmother's. . . . Place called Peaceable, in New Hampshire. . . .

"I know it's an absurd name. . . . Can you make it—tomorrow if possible? Sunday if not? We're leaving Monday, probably early. . . .

"Easy. Just look at a road map; get into town and telephone. Name's Mrs. Samuel Pemberton. I'll expect you. . . .

"Sure there's a motel, but Gran has a big house. . . . 'Bye. Be seeing you."

Jenny shook her short curls. She had this year decided against long hair. "Makes me look masculine," she'd said. "I must say you aren't very romantic," she remarked.

"Says who?"

"Me. . . . Are you serious about Mac?"

"Everyone's serious about everyone, for as long as it lasts. I'm serious enough to have found a summer job in Boston . . . he's working there. He gets paid; I won't be, but at least we can have the summer together. I haven't told Mom yet."

"What about when you go back to Blue Mountain?"

"We'll be seniors," said Viki, "and there's very little time for fun, games, and private lives."

13

"I don't get it. I thought you didn't like guys your age."

"Age is relative. I'll be twenty. Mac was twenty-one a few weeks ago."

"Wow!" Jenny remarked. "An older man!"

"He's a lot more mature than I am. I simply made college a little earlier—all that Country Day emphasis on high grades, to say nothing of the summer work Dad insisted on. He wanted a brace of eager beavers. Look at you; you'll be at Blue Mountain at seventeen, just as I was. Sometimes I think it's a mistake. . . . Mrs. L. is ringing her chimes."

She opened a door, called, "Edna . . . lunch."

Edna responded, bewildered, "I don't know where the morning's gone," and scampered off, willing and scatterbrained.

Viki, throwing things into a tote bag, thought: Mac will come to Peaceable. I know he will. Gran will like him. Mom will have her usual reservations and demand a dossier: Where were you born? What's your ancestry? What do your parents do? What are you going to do? And, probably: What are your intentions? Talk about Victorian! . . . How she got that way, God knows.

A little later, running downstairs, carrying tote bag and a transistor, she thought: I'll break it to the Parent after we get to Gran's . . . and I can't wait to tell Mac the Boston job is all set. She hadn't told anyone else except Jenny.

Her heartbeat was like a little drum, insistent, challenging. She thought: All summer—and Mac. . . . After that, everything will change.

14

 2

CYNTHIA, IN THE DRIVER'S SEAT of her elegant and costly car, brought around by Fred while the family was at lunch, regarded Viki, who leaned in at the window. She thought, quite objectively: She's an unusual-looking girl—very little makeup. No hairdo—just, I suppose soap, water, brush and comb, plus the unsubtle eye stuff, and her curiously colored lipstick. She gets the long lashes from my mother, the red hair from both her father and me. Jenny's more like me. She said aloud, "Fred brought up your car. But it's silly, each of us driving up alone."

Viki suggested, with obvious reluctance, "If you'd really rather, I'll come with you."

She thought: Cooped up with Mom all those miles, trying to think and unable to. She'll have the cassette or the radio going and she'll ask questions. Even if she doesn't, she'll talk.

"No, I'll be all right. Thank you."

Viki's face was pure sunlight. "Well, good. I sort of like to be free . . . to go where I please. And I might want to come home before you, or even stay on a day or so," she said.

"When will you get to Peaceable, approximately?"

"I haven't the least idea. I want to make a stop or two on the way. The music shop here in town—I'll take Gran some new records. And going into Peaceable there's that antique shop—you know—'Crazy Quilt.' They sometimes have things I can use and I like to bargain."

"Are you going via the Thruway?"

"No. Back roads as much as possible—no trucks, no noise, which I hate."

"That's hard to believe," said her mother.

"Traffic noises and rock are a little different. I can't shut traffic out because the VW isn't air-conditioned. Tell Gran to keep dinner in the oven; I'll be along." She leaned closer to offer her smooth cheek, which Cynthia brushed with her lips lightly. "I hope Jenny will be all right," she said.

"Why not? The Owens are dull but reliable; Florence is straight as a drink; and there are always the horses. You keep forgetting that Jenny will be more or less on her own come September."

CYNTHIA TOOK THE COUNTRY ROAD into town and out to the Thruway. She thought irritably that it was incredible that she had daughters—one who would soon enter her senior year and the other her freshman. She hadn't much approved of Blue Mountain. She would have preferred to have the girls attend the older, more conservative—well, not so conservative now of course—institution from which she and her mother had graduated. But Viki had set the example for Jenny by refusing. She'd been accepted there and at other colleges—"All too big," she said. "Who wants to be a statistic?" and her father had agreed with her. Edward almost always agreed with his children. He'd laid down some basic ground rules, and insisted that these be kept; beyond that he went along.

Don't think of Edward. . . .

Yet the main reason for this impulsive trip was to be able to think of him, away from the house, the girls, the neighbors, the club, the routine. What had happened? All she knew was the woman's name, that she had some sort of a job on a fashion magazine and lived alone—and available— in the city.

The second time around; the second open break. How many times had there been rounds which he'd managed to keep from her during the past nine years?

A good, careful driver, one portion of Cynthia's mind was fixed upon roads, turns, signs, lights, the cars which passed and the cars in back of her . . . but the important part was on other matters. She would not think now of last night— the degrading, wretched scene, and eventually, sleep with the help of pills, and Edward in the bed next to hers.

"I'll sleep in a guest room."

"No . . . the girls will hear you."

"They've already heard us, and what the hell dif- ference would my going down the hall make?"

Then, crying uncontrollably, she stumbled to the bath- room for the pills. When she came back, he was in the other bed, turned away from her. She did not know whether or not he slept because, shortly, she was engulfed in the creeping warm fog, blotting out memory, merciful and insidious.

When she had awakened, her head ached. Remem- bering was pitiless sun after fog. Edward's bed was empty. He was not in the dressing room. She heard Viki, and Jenny, who'd gone clattering downstairs with the dog Maisie at her heels. They were going to breakfast. She got up, showered, dressed, did what she could for her face and eyes, and then went down to June brilliance, Viki pouring warm coffee, Jenny scolding Maisie, Edward drinking coffee, looking with irritation at his newspaper and with indulgence at his children. "Good morning, everyone," Cynthia said brightly. "I overslept. . . . Jenny, can't you do something about your hair?"

"Like what?"

"Like brushing it."

Viki, sitting in her mother's place, said, "Sorry to have taken over, but Dad wants out."

Sure, he wants out, thought Cynthia and her jaw tightened. Well, he couldn't have it. She had been and was a good wife; there was no fault or blemish in her; she had given him no cause; none whatever.

Mrs. Larsen looked in to inquire how she wanted her eggs. She didn't want eggs, thank you; just juice and toast; and "Coffee, please, Viki; black."

"You dieting?" asked Jenny, who watched her weight.

"Not really."

So there they'd sat the four of them, the Family, and Jenny rattled on, thank heaven, making conversation to which the others rarely listened, and Viki spoke now and then to her father. "Any news? I forgot to turn my radio on this morning."

"A plethora," he'd answered; "all of it bad."

Cynthia drank the hot black coffee and crumbled some toast. The juice didn't want to go down. She'd risen after a moment, saying, "Excuse me. I forgot my list for Mrs. Larsen." She had left the room, unhurried physically, but inwardly straining to run and hide.

Once in her own room, she'd stood by the bedroom window to see and hear Edward drive away.

Now she halted at a stop sign. She'd told herself not to remember last night or this morning. But she had remembered. She thought: And the first time?

Nine years ago: The worn-out cliché discoveries, the lack of awareness even when he had stayed at the Club many

18

nights. The office had been very busy nine years ago, a great deal busier than now. Then the telephone call. The girls had been upstairs, Jenny long since asleep; they still had Bessie then to look after them. Mrs. Larsen was in her quarters and whoever was in Edna's more lowly position, in hers. Cynthia was reading a novel recommended by her friends, but one she thought revolting, however well reviewed. Edward was in the library which served not only to house books but as his home office. Cynthia heard the telephone ring on his desk, and as the door was open, his end of a brief conversation.

"Hello?" he said and then, cool and guarded, "No, I'm sorry. . . . No, it's not possible. . . . I'm working this evening. My wife and I are here alone. . . . Yes, of course. . . . I'll get back to you tomorrow. . . . Good-bye."

When he came out of the library, he'd said, "That oaf——"

"What oaf?" she'd asked, not caring.

"Barton's son. We hired him last month. He should know better than to call me here."

And all she'd thought was: What an odd thing for him to say: "My wife and I are here alone."

After that, the lipstick stain, a color she didn't use; and the scent, which she didn't use either, and her twice-divorced friend, reporting at lunch with wide-eyed innocence:

"I went to a new place last night, with a new man, thank God. It's a sort of dark, expensive hole in the wall but, as usual, my escort couldn't afford to be seen with me, and who was over in the corner but Edward, with a very good-looking, quite young woman. They were talking, you might say, intensely. Don't tell me Edward's hit the trail. I can't believe it!" She'd sighed and ordered another drink, at which Cynthia had shaken her head, saying, "Not for me. I rarely have even one at lunch."

19

"Of course. Our resident paragon. . . . I suppose you knew all about Edward and his date last night?"

"Certainly."

Last night Edward had been dining with clients.

So what had she done then? She had suffered in silence, wept in solitude, entertained guests, accomplished whatever charity work she was doing at the time, overseen the household, including the children and their Bessie, and felt her pride being stripped from her as painfully as if it had been her skin.

Inevitably, what is now called "the confrontation," with Edward slamming off to the Club, and Cynthia herself making the excuses: Mr. Warren wouldn't be home for a while, he'd had to go on an unexpected trip. "Mr. Warren" to the domestic help; "Daddy" to the girls; "Edward" to their friends.

But he'd come back; he'd been gone perhaps two weeks.

He'd said that he was sorry; that he'd been an ass; that he didn't expect her to forgive him but that she knew he loved her and their girls.

Strange that at that time she hadn't thought of going to her mother. There was a reason; her father had been dead for only a year.

Battling her way strategically through the Friday-afternoon traffic—it would be worse before it became better —she thought that if her father had been alive, it would have been easy to go to him.

It was her parents' example, she thought, with self-pity and anger. You grew up expecting that when you married, your marriage would be like theirs: the single-minded absorption; the absurd private jokes; the lively interest each took in whatever the other said and did; the funny little quarrels which flared up and then subsided, usually in laughter. Not that they weren't fond of and devoted to their children—to her, Cynthia, and to Jack—in her mother's case, especially to Jack. And when Jack was killed, her mother had had a shoulder to lean on, a hand to hold, a man to share with her this shattering loss.

Edward and I have never shared anything, she thought.

How had she met him? At a cocktail party in New York. She was out of college and had her first and only paying job, in the Research Library firm involved with—of all things—the oil industry. Her employer was a friend of her father's.

Edward had been in the army, and upon his release he'd gone to work in the advertising agency his uncle had founded. She'd thought, standing with him in the drawing room of one of her classmates' parents, that he was one of the handsomest men she'd ever seen; tall, wide in the shoulders, narrow at waist and hips, thick coppery hair, and bright brown eyes. His mother told her later that he'd been a bricktop as a child, "but he's toned down," she'd added. She died shortly after their return from the wedding trip to Jamaica. Cynthia had liked her; a quiet, intelligent widow, who had, without the usual hand wringing, relinquished her only child to another woman.

They had left Jamaica when Edward's uncle cabled that Mrs. Warren was going into the hospital for tests, and possibly exploratory surgery. Flying home, anxious about Edward's mother and sorry for Edward, Cynthia was relieved to be away from the soft beguiling tropics, the incredibly clear warm water, the curving beach, the languor and seductiveness. She was relieved to have escaped the drifting days; the bright strangers who talked, laughed, and drank with them; the drives into the mountains; the glimpses of waterfalls, of native children; the night clubs, shops, calypsos, steel drums, and singing.

Possibly because always—in the dawn or after swimming, sometimes in the afternoons with the blinds lowered, and of course in the night, scented with flowers haunted by music coming from somewhere—there was the aromatic breeze permeating the bedroom she shared too often with her husband.

Before their marriage, during the short engagement, it had been exciting, flattering, and even a little touching to watch him struggle for control, to hear him say, "But, darling, we're going to be married," or the worn words which uncounted millions have spoken in all languages, "I love you so much; I want you so much."

All this had moved her to a response part vanity, part curiosity, part knowledge that she held the cards; and also partly a belief that, after they were married, she would experience the fulfillment that she'd read about and had heard young women discuss with appalling frankness.

In Jamaica this had not happened; she had approached the edge of desire by slow, pleasurable stages, and then retreated. It wasn't my fault, she told herself now; it wasn't my fault.

Edward's. . . ?

Don't think about Jamaica, and the slow painful tears, after he slept. . . .

After Jamaica, the years of settling into routine; it was all routine: a house, servants, a husband home from the office, children. . . . She'd had, even with Viki, a remarkably easy time, or so they told her. Not that easy, she'd told herself. Entertaining had become routine . . . and the shared bedroom. She had been faithful to routine. She had met all her obligations; she had denied them nothing; not her house, her friends, her children, or her husband. She could lie in bed with Edward and think her own thoughts; occasionally they were that the double bed of her early marriage had been a monumental mistake but that twin beds also had drawbacks; they were too narrow for comfort. She could think about new curtains or what was to be done in the garden, or that Jenny was getting impertinent or that she must have the Harleys for dinner, much as she disliked Mrs. Harley. But Edward liked her—the shallow, pretty woman, always conscious of her effect upon men.

Sex. . . . Nine years ago Edward had told her, "Men get into situations like this, very often because they feel wanted and needed. No matter how much I love you—and I still do—you have never wanted or needed me."

After he came home, she'd tried to express her gratitude for his return by a welcoming and a warmth. Tried— and almost succeeded. The intimacy which was so alien to her mind—more so than to her docile body—had not been too difficult because, in its way, it was a victory; and for every victory the victor pays a price.

This time, however, was different. They were nine years older . . . and Edward wanted a divorce. He loved someone else. "Not just in love," he had explained to her last night. "I don't love you, Cynthia; I did for a long time. Or thought I did."

Her life—and her routine—were as fragmented as the T'ang horse. The house, the household, the children, the security, the stability, the superior pride—through which she could regard tolerably her friends who married and remarried, who had affairs, who came whining to her with their problems—husbands, lovers, money. "You're always serene, Cynthia; so sensible. Tell me what to do."

Who would tell her what to do? What could she do, except refuse him a divorce? Even if he went from the Club

23

to another state, she could fight; she would fight. She had been faithful in body and mind. She had kept his house; she had been an integral part of his success; she had interested herself in his profession, been gracious and pleasant to his friends; she had brought up their children admirably; she never barred Edward from his marital rights. She had forgiven him the episode of almost a decade ago. She had taught herself not to speculate how many unimportant episodes had followed. Unimportant to her—as long as she didn't know about them; as long as there were no scenes, no open breach. Women attracted him; she'd realized that even in Jamaica. But he had always come back to her. Convinced of her non-knowledge, although feeling guilty for a time, like a man who has had several drinks too many and is hung over, feeling sick and sorry and telling himself, "Never again."

Why am I going to my mother's? I've never really known her. . . . Oh, she's fond of me, I suppose, but she's never really liked me, Cynthia thought. But she likes Edward. He flatters her, teases her, amuses her. But she'll try to be impartial.

If it weren't for Viki, off on her own somewhere but bound to turn up at Peaceable, she would have been tempted to go to a motel and spend the night alone; or even to return to her house, with any excuse, such as saying, "Suddenly I didn't feel well. I must be coming down with something. I just want to go to bed. . . ." And then she'd ask, she wouldn't be able to help asking, "Is there a message from Mr. Warren?"

She'd gone too far to turn back.

When finally she took the little road which led into Peaceable, she looked at it only because she must, driving a car. Beyond the small town the textile factory, which her father had dominated until his retirement, was still—through the shares she had inherited—her mother's main source of

24

income, and also provided Cynthia and her children with personal incomes.

Out, through the familiar town and up a hill; around a winding road and up another hill. . . . It's hell in winter, Cynthia thought crossly. . . . Then the big elderly house, of no particular architecture; the house in which she had been born, in which she'd grown up, from which she had gone on journeys and to college; and to which, after her wedding in her parents' church, she had returned for the reception in the big living room, filled with flowers, faces, laughter, the smell of roses and cigarettes and women's perfume; filled with the light and presence of June.

She was suddenly shaken to realize that the anniversary of that wedding fell on the coming Sunday. She had said to Edward almost a month ago; "What do you want to do on our anniversary? Have some people in? Take them out? Or perhaps just go to New York, the two of us?" And he answered, "Suppose we decide later."

Back in Westchester, wrapped and tied, in a dresser drawer was her present for him. Cuff links this time. At others it had been a batch of ties, or something for golf or fishing, or monogrammed shirts or handkerchiefs, a new billfold, a money clip—whatever it was, it had been routine, like his to her, although for the first few years his gifts had been especially designed for her.

He'd said to her once, "I like the ties very much, but I wish you'd give me something a little crazy for my birthday or Christmas or our anniversary."

"What do you mean crazy?" she'd asked, laughing. "You sound like Viki, always saying, 'I love it; it's crazy!'"

"Well . . . perhaps, I meant imaginative."

"You know I've no imagination," she'd said soberly.

"Yes, I know."

She was glad she hadn't; it wouldn't have served her

well nine years ago or now. . . . Even if you haven't experienced something, you could—or so she'd heard—imagined it.

She drove up to the house and stopped.

Lucy Pemberton came down the veranda steps, as Cynthia emerged from the car, reaching for her small suitcase.

"Hi," said her mother. "I've put you and Edward as usual in your bedroom." She stopped, and asked, "Where is Edward?"

"Away for the weekend. . . . You look well, Mother."

Going up the steps, Lucy said, astonished, "But Sunday's your anniversary. . . . I planned a little dinner, after you phoned—just a few old friends."

"Sorry about that," Cynthia said. "It couldn't be helped."

"And where's Viki?"

"On her way . . . in her own car; she said she wanted to poke around. I meant to bring you some of that special tea you fancy, but I didn't stop in the village. Besides this was a spur-of-the-moment trip. Perhaps Viki will remember."

There were sounds from the back of the house and Reba Jones came out, smiling. "Sight for sore eyes," she remarked, putting her arm around Cynthia. Reba was a distant cousin of Sam Pemberton, Cynthia's father. A long spare spinster, white hair, blue eyes, gaunt and agile. She had kept house for the Pembertons for a long time; she was company for Lucy, but—by her own decision—absented herself from the dining room if guests were present, unless they were family. She ruled the house with a thrifty, ruthless efficiency; hiring a competent cook, temporary help when needed. They were local and didn't sleep in. These changed, as did the yard man, but Reba did not.

"Edward didn't come?" she asked Cynthia.

"He couldn't; he has to be away."

"Well," said Reba, "I'll tell Sadie. Isn't Viki coming?"

"She's driving up; she'll be here sometime or other; she said to keep dinner warm."

"Kids," Reba remarked with resignation.

"Come on up," Lucy said and preceded Cynthia and her suitcase. Broad stairs, broad hall, wide enough to be furnished. Lucy's room was on the southwest corner; Cynthia's looked north.

Lucy and Cynthia were not much alike. Lucy was slightly taller than her daughter. She had kept her figure—a little fuller than when she and Sam were young, but still very good. She carried herself beautifully, owing to disciplinary parents. Her skin was fine, softly colored, almost golden; she was out of doors a great deal, summers here, winters now in Florida. Her eyes were blue-gray, and her hair, cut short, was a beautiful pewter.

"Well," said Lucy as Cynthia put her case on a luggage rack and looked around at her room, which hadn't changed a great deal except for new chintz curtains and slipcovers, "you haven't been here since autumn."

"I know."

Last Christmas Lucy had come to Westchester to stay over the New Year on her way to Florida's west coast, where she had friends and to which she had been going for the past eight years.

"Is anything wrong?"

"Of course not."

"Good. Get washed up or whatever and come on down; there's plenty of time. . . . Drink? . . . Tea?"

"Drink, thanks."

"We're having an easy dinner, and we'll wait for Viki. By the way she had a telephone call half an hour ago. Reba took it. Someone who said his name was Mac and that he'd phone again. Who's that?"

27

"I haven't the least idea. Oh, yes . . . Viki did speak to me about someone she called Mac. I didn't pay much attention. There are dozens of them—boys, I mean—and Jenny's beginning to take an interest too. She's past the movie star, TV-personality stage, but she's still horse crazy. Now, however, there are boys. Up till last year she ignored them, despite the fact the Country Day is co-ed."

LUCY WENT DOWNSTAIRS and into the smaller of the two living rooms. The fireplace was filled with birch logs, for looks; the furniture was a mixture of periods, all good. Everything was polished, the woods, the brasses. Sam's desk stood there and in the corner the bar he had amused himself building; he had been skilled with his hands. "Come from an old line of carpenters," he'd tell his guests. He'd liked a drink before dinner, and occasionally a nightcap. Alcohol didn't agree with Lucy, but Sam had kept her supplied with sherry, Dubonnet, Campari.

There was no picture of him in here. He had said, when his wife suggested that his portrait hang over the fireplace, "It would give me the creeps. Who in hell wants to look at himself, especially as that clown Goddard saw me."

"Bill's a very good painter."

"Okay—so I had it done for your birthday. Waste of time and money, but as long as you like it . . ."

The portrait hung now over the fireplace in the larger living room: Sam at his desk, surrounded by books.

On her way to the kitchen, Lucy wandered into this room to look at the portrait. It was certainly Sam, but in a fixed mood; and he'd never had fixed moods. She thought, as she had ever since Viki's birth: She looks like him, the forehead, nose, the mouth.

She wished Viki would come. Cynthia had lied; a social lie of course. But something was wrong. Lucy was aware of it as she was always aware of thunder before a coming storm, even while the sky was still blue and smiling. Perhaps, later on, Cynthia would tell her what it was all about; or she might never. She kept herself to herself. Like me, that way, thought Lucy, except where Sam was concerned.

She was glad Viki was coming. Viki was young, and Lucy liked young people of her own or someone else's blood. They gave her vigor, mental and physical. In time Jenny would; thus far she wasn't interested in Jenny. As for Cynthia . . . Lucy shook her handsome head and thought uneasily: I hope Viki isn't having trouble on the road.

 *3*

VIKI WAS NOT HAVING TROUBLE on the road. Like her mother she was a careful driver; but she enjoyed driving, which Cynthia did not.

When Viki reached town, she found a parking space for the Volkswagen. This was one of her talents which infuriated her mother and father; Viki always managed a parking space; she might have to go twice around the block, but just as she came round again, a car would obligingly back out. "Shot with luck," Edward would comment enviously. No one knew that Viki had a secret weapon.

As a small girl, eleven or twelve, she had been hopelessly in love with one of the town's police officers. Endowed with Irish charm, and having kids of his own, he had a special feeling for them. Shopping with her mother or perhaps Mrs. Larsen, Viki would remain outside on the curb to talk with Casey. Her uncomplicated devotion was not guilt-ridden because Casey was married; she felt for him a simple admiration, and he never talked down to her. By the time she was thirteen, she'd become aware of boys a little older than herself; but Casey retained her affection. When he was killed that year on patrol duty, Viki grieved for and missed him and went, together with most of the townspeople, to his funeral Mass.

After she had learned to drive—taught by Fred in the truck around and around the driveway—and had obtained her first license, she used to speak to Casey in her mind. "Casey," she would say, "find me a parking space." When she entered her sophomore year, she was given her Volks . . . and she still talked to Casey.

Jenny had been promised a car when she, too, became a sophomore. She was being taught to drive, by Fred and Viki. But her sister despaired of her; Jenny was too like their father, given to speed, to impatience with the drivers of other cars, and to tailgating.

Viki went into the record shop where she was an old and valued customer. She was looking for Irish Rovers records; her grandmother was particularly fond of unicorns. Having found these, she selected some soft rock and, in deference to Lucy's other preference, Andy Williams and Perry Como.

Then she walked to the gourmet shop, bought Irish tea and candy, looked for handkerchiefs next door, went on to regard the windows of a dress shop, shook her head, traversed her steps, and backed the Volkswagen into the street.

Her pleasurable duties concluded, she aimed the VW for Peaceable. On such a day, with all the time in the world, it would have been criminal to take to the highways except when you had to. Secondary and country roads would give her scented air, the rustle of leaves, long meadows, rough fields, stone walls, and a sense of utter freedom.

So she had time to think about Mac.

He was a year older than she. He'd worked a full year before entering the freshman class. She had not noticed him much, that first year; Blue Mountain was not a large college as colleges go, but that freshman class had been a big one. And they were not headed toward the same majors. She knew

31

who Mac was; she ran into him occasionally—once, she remembered, in the college radio station where she'd gone to collect Linda and where Mac was busy arguing with one of the working students, a junior. She'd seen him also in the main cafeteria, or one of the small, more interesting college-run places where students met to eat and talk. She encountered him on campus, in halls and classrooms, and now and then in the library. He impressed her only as a big, rather hulking young man, with an interesting and, for his age, curiously battered face, set in graver lines than his years warranted.

In her sophomore year, having moved to a dorm which had little or no supervision, except for a junior counselor, Viki was soon caught up in various programs controlled by the Activities Board. Her major was sociology and the winter term found her working in Boston; her project, helping in a neighborhood community center. Mac was also in Boston working in a science center, his major being environmental studies. She saw him briefly during the winter carnival and at the spring weekend dance, where almost everyone wore costumes of their own wild designing—but not Mac. He danced with her, to her mild astonishment, and they exchanged views on the winter term as if each had been on another planet.

Blue Mountain was country-minded. When you could, you got away for a weekend; in the winter there were always groups for skiing, and later for hiking and camping. That spring Viki went camping with Linda and a dozen of their classmates, including boys—and Mac.

Around a campfire, on a night brilliant with stars and chilly with wind, she sat beside Mac and they talked. Many of the male students with common interests had got together and rented a house, a sort of club—there were no longer fraternities as such—but Mac explained that he couldn't afford it. "Thank God for the scholarship. My parents can't help. There are five of us kids; I'm the oldest. Ever since I can remember

I've worked summers—paper route, errand running, grass cutting, until I was old enough to have a regular job; and I always saved. . . . I don't suppose you have to worry about bread."

"No," she'd admitted, "but what makes you think so?"

"I dunno. Just . . . you haven't the look. Tell me about yourself."

"Not much to tell . . . mother, father, younger sister, place in Westchester."

He nodded. "That figures. Country club, riding, private school—and, of course, your car."

"What's wrong with that? Is it all too Establishment for your taste?"

"Don't get mad."

"I'm not."

"I've nothing against the System. If I could, I'd make a lot of changes in it, and I hope to try someday, by being part of it. Outsiders can change it some—they already have—but it's the insiders who can really make it work and a damned lot better than now." He shook his head. "Most protests are just noise," he said after a minute, "and burning schools gets you nowhere fast, and bomb throwing is for the guys who have to —poor bastards! I've seen a lot of riots and heard a lot of yelling. Sure, sometimes it does some good; but usually it's without much direction—and to fight violence with violence is as stupid as some wars."

"His draft status?" she'd wondered aloud.

"Well, I've a deferment. I hope this doesn't change before I graduate. I can't sincerely be a C.O.," he added, as sparks leaped from the logs and a tall flame illuminated briefly his half-serious, half-smiling face and the mop of curling brown hair. "I'm against killing, as most decent people are. But when it's in self-defense, or defense of property or of other people's lives, or in defense of this country, if circumstances warrant, I couldn't object on religious grounds; it wouldn't be true. And I can't claim moral or ethical grounds because I think it's really just sheer revulsion."

He reached out suddenly and took her hand as another spark sailed out, another flame came briefly to life.

"You're very pretty," was all he said, but it was a beginning.

All through the rest of the term they were together as much as possible, but she did not see him that summer. He was working at Woods Hole, and couldn't, as he wrote her, afford to get away. And Viki was working in a Rehab Center near her home. She wrote him; she sent him a knotted string belt, beautifully patterned "Macramé for Mac" she explained in the note that went with it. "I know a guy who makes these. Wear it in good health. Every day."

So all summer she remembered holding hands in the movies, walking with his arm around her shoulder, kissing, not talking very much.

"You're not ready to get totally involved are you, Viki?"

"No."

"I don't know that I am either."

"Have you ever been, Mac?"

"Not that much; no."

That was the evening after an hour or so at the place which served coffee and Danish and had a jukebox. It closed before eleven, so they had walked to the students' parking lot and taken the VW out and, with Mac at its wheel, had driven through the woods and stopped on a hill where there was a valley view. It was a favored spot for students, but that night no one else was there. She'd ridden along quiet and content, her head against his shoulder and had said, after they were parked, "I'm glad you're much taller . . ."

To her horror, after he had kissed her, she began to

34

cry. And he had asked troubled, "What's the matter, Viki?"

"Sorry," she said, mopping her face. "Maybe it's my name."

"Are you out of your skull?" he demanded, running his hand roughly over her hair, feeling the skull shape beneath.

"No. I was named Victoria."

He'd laughed then. "There aren't too many of them left," he said, "the Victorians, especially at our age."

She'd said slowly, "I just want to be sure. . . . I suppose I won't see you this summer."

"Nope. I can't afford it; the best I can do is go home one or two weekends."

"I'll think about you and—involvement," she promised. "All summer. Then we'll be back at school, and by then, I'll be sure."

"One way or another?"

"That's it. You too, Mac?"

"Right on," he said absently. "You might meet a guy. I might meet a gal. And if we don't, there are things to think about."

"Such as?"

"Such as not getting married. I can't afford it."

She said, "If it came to that, I have some money of my own."

"Nuts to that. And then there's the draft; deferments don't go on forever; even if I went to grad school, which I can't afford either."

She said suddenly, "Come to think of it, I don't want to get married!"

"Why?"

"I'm too young. I haven't enough sense."

He had laughed again and kissed her, and after a while they went back to the campus.

Walking her to her dorm from the parking lot, he'd said, "We have next year. . . ."

Neither said anything about the year after that, the rat race of the senior.

So she'd thought all summer and presumably so had he, according to his letters, remarkably articulate for a man not ordinarily so. And she could hardly wait for the autumn term to open.

She had worked hard, and with very knowledgeable people, at the Center, which was for young addicts, and she was torn with revulsion and compassion. She knew some of the patients who came to the Center—it was not in her town, but near by—and she knew of their families. Mostly she answered telephones, gave information, kept records, and was permitted sometimes to sit in with her superiors on the talk sessions.

She was completely aware of drugs, up and down the scale; there wasn't a college in the country, or a high school— possibly not even an elementary school, public or private— which didn't have the problem. Linda had gone through a mild stage, and recovered; her second trial trip had frightened her. Now Linda was straight, but at that first try she had tried to convert Viki: "Can't do any harm to try. It's great. You're missing something." But Viki had felt no necessity, no pressure, and no need to conform. Most of her friends were straight, as Linda had been except for the brief lapse; and so was Mac. He and Viki had talked about that too.

He'd said that a number of things turned him on (herself for instance). Things you could really dig—music, people who gave you something to think about, books you could read more than once. "The world—I'd like to see every place in it before I die—the planet, and beyond. I don't want to be turned on by anything else. Oh, I like a drink now and then, but not too much of that. I was completely stoned once; it didn't agree with me. Being out of control is humiliating. . . . And I'm turned on by what I've learned. I'm above average, they tell me, but not enough to set the world on fire. As a matter of fact I'm against setting the world on fire; literally, that is. It makes me vomit to see and smell what's been done to this country—to all the environment. Maybe we're too late. I dunno, but we can damned well give it a try.

"They say that drugs give you an expanding consciousness and a spiritual awareness." He added something short and descriptive, and then laughed. "Sorry about that. If I'm so set on cleaning up the earth, I'd better start with my own language. . . . Well, thanks," he concluded. "I find my consciousness—if that's what it is—expands like crazy as things are, and my awareness too, although I doubt it's spiritual."

Darling Mac, she thought, remembering.

Next year she'd graduate, provided she wasn't felled by leprosy or something equally dire. There'd be no sweat over her marks; she liked working and was fortunate in her teachers. There was only one she felt was bored with her classes, but if you had any sense, you ignored it, because boredom is contagious. But Viki would always think of her junior year as her graduation; even when she was middle-aged; when she was old, with a flock of grandchildren around her. The odds were on that because someday she would marry someone. She wondered a little where he was now, who he was, where he lived, in love with someone or out of it, working, going to school? His name might not be Paul McDonald. A sudden quake of sorrow, a wave of loss, a shiver of desire shook her. Where would Mac be then, light years from now? Quick or dead? Married? With children, grandchildren?

She laughed, stopping at a crossroad and a man driving a big car halted beside her, looking at the girl with the long red hair and the laughing mouth. "What's funny?" he inquired, leaning out, but Viki merely waved, smiled, and went her way.

Nothing was funny . . . everything was funny . . . and mysterious.

Her real graduation had not been academic, but emotional and physical . . . laced with wonder, fringed with curiosity, clouded at first with anxiety. She had not been innocent of responses; there had been others before Mac; curtain raisers, prologues; but she had to be sure; and she'd never been until the summer—last summer—which had separated her from Mac.

From the moment they'd met again on campus everything was all right. The first casual hi, the first touch, the first questioning glance. They had some weekends, hiking in woods starting to shout with color, and in the winter they'd gone to one of the nearby ski places—she skiied, he didn't. "Too expensive" he'd said, "and think of the medical bills in addition!" But usually she went, if feasible, to his room. It was small, austerely furnished, and he lived in it alone.

That year they talked endlessly; rap sessions with Mac flat on the bed, Viki curled up in the one big shabby chair. What had they talked about? Often after returning home she had tried to reproduce the conversation in her mind, but couldn't—war and peace, love, sex, politics, injustice, old novels, poetry, music, always music. She gave him before Christmas, a small player and records he especially liked. And he gave her a little gold locket with a diamond chip set in the middle of the heart. It had belonged to his grandmother, who had left it to him. Viki wore it hidden by turtleneck sweaters, or under Mexican blouses or shirts. The thin chain was long. The locket rested between her pretty breasts. She wore it at night, in the dorm, and at home. Linda thought she was nuts. "You're wasting your time," said Linda, who, having wasted hers happily with quite a few guys, was helpful and sympathetic. "Can you afford to get pregnant?" she had inquired.

Last Christmas Linda had spent a few days of her vacation with the Warrens, coming up from the South, and going on to Pennsylvania before returning to school. At home, on Christmas Eve, Linda had met SOMEONE at a friend's house. She spoke of the meeting in capital letters. "Finally," she said, in her quick, light voice. He was from the North, and working in a big company which had a branch in her home city. From then on, Linda no longer played the field.

During Linda's stay in Westchester, Viki had given a party for her, and included her friends, those of her classmates who lived near, all the young men she could muster, including Mac and his cousin. Mac's cousin, Allen, was older; he worked in New York and had a car. So they'd driven up, and spent the evening, dancing, eating, talking, drinking, mostly beer. Jenny had darted from one group to the other, beside herself with excitement. The older Warrens had remained in the house, having learned from other parents' experience that it was the wiser course. "None of this crap about the kids don't want us around," Edward had said to his wife. "We'll be there."

They were unobtrusive; they simply drifted into the big family room now and then, shouting pleasantries over the music, sampling Mrs. Larsen's buffet, and drifting out again.

Mac had approved of them. He'd said, "So, they keep an eye on you, Viki."

"They can't always," she said gravely, but her dark eyes laughed with him.

This morning—was it this morning? It seemed so long ago—she'd mentioned Mac to her mother, but Cynthia hadn't remembered him. Of course she'd been in no mood to remember anything except the night before; she'd been hung over with shock and anger and hurt. But Edward recalled Mac. He'd asked about him when Viki was home in the spring. "That—what was his name?—McDonald boy. He still in school?"

"Oh, you remember him?"

"Of course, we had a short talk; he's okay. Who was the other one, the one he brought with him?"

"Mac's cousin. He lives in New York."

"Where's Mac from?"

"Boston."

"I liked him," said her father. "Big quiet chap, seems to know where he's going. I take it you like him too?"

"Oh, yes," she'd said lightly. "He's my current guy."

"Seriously?"

"For the time being; but it isn't fatal."

She'd been conscious of her father's searching rather somber look, and had thought: Men who like women are more suspicious, maybe, than the fathers who stick to the beaten path—office, home, office, home, country club. She wondered how many of these she knew—not many she imagined—and her father, as she'd learned nine years ago, and again today, was not one of them.

If Dad knew . . . she thought. God knows he must be aware of the world around him. But he tried for the middle road, lenient, but not permissive. As for her mother, she'd have a stroke if . . .

Viki began to worry. Perhaps she had been out of her mind to ask—beg, was more like it—Mac to come to Peacable. But she had to talk to him about the Boston caper. She'd written him that she'd applied for the job, and again when she'd been accepted, which was very recently. She couldn't talk about it over the phone. She must manage to be alone with him at her grandmother's. She'd be careful and tell Mac to be too. "It's Gran's house," she'd remind him, "and my mother's also in it. I've a thing about—well, other people's houses. . . . I would have about yours, for instance."

She wondered briefly what her grandmother would say if she became aware. Lucy Pemberton was seventy . . . fifty years ahead of—or was it behind?—her granddaughter. Viki loved her. Lucy Pemberton was tops.

Well, a step at a time. Pretty soon, she thought, I'll be in Boston. Next term things had to be different; not that she and Mac wouldn't see each other, if "the summer," as she termed it to herself, proved out; but not as much, not as often. They couldn't. In her three college years she'd seen seemingly obsessed couples break up—and only a few go on to marry after graduation.

She drove into Peaceable and stopped to talk to one of her favorite people, Dan, who owned a gas station and considerable land, and who was an important figure at Town Meetings. His boy was a freshman at Blue Mountain.

"My mother been by, Dan?"

"Quite a while back; she didn't stop; just waved. How come you're alone?"

"I like to be free," Viki told him, with her wide smile.

"That's what Dan, Jr., says. Sometimes I worry about him, Viki."

"Don't. He'll be all right. The first year is the hardest; it's a shakedown cruise."

"Staying with us awhile? I know Sara would like you to come to the house."

"I don't know. Haven't made up my mind. But I'll try to stop by. Monday maybe."

"She's always fretting about young Dan, and although you're always welcome, Viki, the fact that you are on the same campus and breathing the same air—which I take it is still pretty good—would make you doubly so, to Sara."

Viki said carelessly, "I expect a gorgeous boy friend,

tomorrow. He'll probably pull up here and ask directions. He's never been in town."

"Okay. . . . What's his name?"

"Paul McDonald. Mac, for short."

"If I don't take to him, I'll misdirect him, but good."

She went away laughing and Dan stood watching her for a moment; he'd known her since she was knee-high. I'd better like him, he thought.

Viki stopped at the Crazy Quilt, steamed in, and greeted its two owners, maiden ladies of indefinite age. They embraced her and one said, "You've grown!"

"God forbid. . . . It's just that you haven't seen me for a spell."

She hunted in the big leather bag swung from her shoulder. "I am down to my last dime," she said. "What shall I blow it on?"

There was a brass candlestick she liked, and for her grandmother a cup plate in the tea-leaf pattern. She fished out some bills. "Richer than I thought," she announced, paid for her purchases, said "Good-bye . . . be seeing you" and headed for the Pemberton house . . . wondering, and somewhat anxious, about her mother. Has she told Gran? Will she tell her?

Wondering, too, about Mac. Suppose he didn't come?

 *4*

VIKI CANTERED IN, her tote bag pregnant with packages, and called, crossing the threshold, "Anyone home?"

"We're here and starving." Lucy Pemberton came from the study, quick as a minnow. Cynthia had not inherited her mother's fluid, easy movements; but Viki had.

"Sorry." Viki put her arms around her grandmother. She said, "Hey, you're thin. . . . Dieting?"

Cynthia appeared in the study doorway, "I think your grandmother looks very well," she commented.

"I didn't say she looked unhealthy. I said she's thin."

"Pants suits," explained Lucy, smiling. "I've bought a few; I love them."

Cynthia, who owned numerous pants suits, looked a trifle disapproving, but Viki hugged her grandmother again. "That's my girl," she said. "Gran, I'm sorry I'm late."

"You're not, really. Run upstairs—I've put you next to me—and wash your face; it's smudged."

"Mascara. I cried all the way here," Viki said blandly. She dumped all but one of the packages on her grandfather's desk. "Tea," she said, "records, and a cup plate. Oh, and a box of candy for Reba, and some wild handkerchiefs for Sadie. . . . See you later."

She went upstairs with her light, sure step, and into the designated bedroom, hung up a few things, went into the small bathroom to wash her face and put on lipstick. She looked around her happily. Things didn't change here; well . . . they had, somewhat, after Grandfather died. But that was long ago, a decade.

Clattering downstairs, she went into the kitchen to embrace Reba, who said, "You don't come often enough. Your grandma misses you, Viki."

"I know. . . . Hi, Sadie, what's for dinner?"

Sadie, middle-aged and rotund, looked doleful. "Not much and maybe spoiled by now, Miss Viki," she answered.

"I don't believe it." Viki went out, laughing, and into the study; there were two empty glasses on the bar. One had contained dry sherry, the other Scotch on the rocks.

"Drinking yourself to death as usual," Viki admonished.

"An orgy," Lucy admitted solemnly. "Sadie's waited so long now, she can wait a little longer. What's your pleasure?" She thought: Sam always said that. I picked it up from him.

"Nothing except food."

Reba joined them and they went into the dining room; big, sunny, and uncluttered. Roses on the servers and on the table. At one time, Viki remembered vaguely, there'd been tons of silver, but Lucy had put most of it away after her husband's death. She wouldn't be entertaining nearly as much as formerly. Who needed silver butter plates and pitchers and all the rest? Besides the constant cleaning? Enough remained in the pantry chests to serve eight, without extra trappings.

Dinner was not spoiled; it was simple and good and the peas were from the garden, also the strawberries.

Lucy said suddenly, "I'd almost forgotten, Viki, but you had a phone call, before your mother came . . . a man——"

44

"Name of Mac?" asked Viki casually.

"That's right. He said he'd call again."

Lucy looked at her granddaughter and thought; I used to look like that, stunned with happiness, radiant with it, for such a long time, and probably several times a day. I'd like to be young and alive, the heart on tiptoe, but only if Sam were young with me.

Viki said, "You mind if Mac comes here tomorrow, maybe, and spends the night, Gran?"

"Of course not. There's Jack's room."

For a long time Lucy had not used Jack's room until Sam had said quietly, "Jack would want it used, dear."

"How's he getting here if he comes?" Cynthia asked, not caring, but making the effort. She frowned a little, remembering. "As I recall it now, he drove up from the city with his cousin last Christmas."

"He has a car now, Mom, secondhand and doubtless beat-up. He bought it from a friend last summer, when he— Mac that is—was going to work at Woods Hole."

After that, Viki did not eat much, the edge of her healthy appetite dulled with anticipation, most of her being concentrated on listening for the telephone.

They were having coffee in the study, and Cynthia had said she was tired, so "just a spot of brandy please," she told her mother. Viki had a mild mint, "for the digestion," she explained gravely. "Besides, I like it. One of my early memories is being here around Thanksgiving, I think, and it was raining, Gramp gave me a box of cream white peppermints and an apple. I lay on my bed, ate peppermints and drank water, chonked on a russet, and read."

They talked about Jenny; they talked about the weather; they talked about college, and Viki thought: Mom hasn't told Gran yet.

The telephone rang and Viki reached it first. She said,

"Yes, I got here late. Gran wants you to stay overnight. . . . You can come tomorrow, can't you?"

She listened a moment, said, "We'll expect you before dinner. When you get to Peaceable, look for Dan's service station. It's on the edge of the village on the main road. He'll tell you how to get here. I've briefed him . . . See you," hung up and reported unnecessarily, "Mac's coming sometime tomorrow afternoon. . . . Thanks, Gran."

"*Por Nada,*" said her grandmother and Viki commented, "You haven't forgotten Spain."

"Nor my three or four Spanish words. I never shall," said Lucy thinking of a rented car and Sam behind the wheel crying, "Look, darling; look, on your side."

That was driving south along the coast to Jávea. They'd been in Valencia for a few nights, at the Astoria Palace, during the holidays of St. Joseph.

"Woolgathering?" inquired Viki, and Lucy said, "No, yellow iris."

Cynthia sighed. Her mother was a thousand miles from being senile, but there were times when she did not understand, or could not follow her. Viki seemed to, for she smiled, raised her little glass, and said, "Okay, I'll drink to yellow iris, Gran."

THEY WENT TO BED EARLY. There was an uneasiness in the atmosphere, a lack of communication of which Lucy was aware. Viki? . . . No. . . . Cynthia? . . . Of course. So she said, "You girls must be tired and I'm sleepy." She wasn't, but she managed to yawn. "I'll go up and read awhile."

So they went, each to her own room and Lucy said mechanically as she had when Jack and Cynthia were young and, after them, Viki and Jenny, "If you need anything, call me."

They said good night and Reba came up to ask

46

Lucy, "Someone else coming? I heard the phone after I left you."

"Just one of Viki's followers," Lucy told her. "He'll be driving up from Boston, and she expects him sometime during the afternoon tomorrow."

"Staying overnight?"

"Yes. We'll put him in Jack's room."

"I saw her face at dinner when you told her he'd phoned." Reba shook her head. "We'll go through this a dozen times with her, and pretty soon with Jenny. Beats all," she said, "the way they grow up. . . . 'Night, Lucy."

Lucy got ready for the night and crawled into bed, sighing a little. It had been so empty for so long and she still felt lost in it. She switched on the FM. The clock radio was on the bedside table; beside it, Sam's picture, the thermos, and the pill she had taken occasionally in recent weeks. She'd be seeing Pete Harmon next Friday. "You be here," he'd told her, and she'd answered, "You're the doctor."

Very few people reach seventy without a twinge now and then, here, there, or another place. A vigorous woman, she had always assured Sam—until he became ill—"I'll live to be a hundred, and so will you." Her contemporaries were subject to aches, pains, chronic disorders; she wasn't. But now she was annoyed by the betrayal of her body, and at Pete. "He's a fusspot," she told herself. "A complete check up? Who needs it?"

He'd said, "Just to be sure, Lucy."

She turned out the bedside lamp and lay back against the pillows listening to the music. Viki probably had her transistor on; it went everywhere with her, a constant companion. Tomorrow I must play the new records, thought Lucy, and after a minute, said, "Good night Sam," and drifted into sleep.

She was a light sleeper and awoke about two in the

morning. Her radio had long since obligingly turned itself off. She looked at the illuminated clock, and then switched on the lamp. Something had awakened her; but the house was still and there were no sounds except leaves rustling beyond the open windows.

She rose, opened the bedroom door, and listened. She had very acute hearing. There was a sound after all; it came from downstairs.

Lucy put on a robe and slippers, and switched on the stairway light. An intruder? She wasn't afraid of anything . . . well—not of very much. She didn't like rodents or snakes, but she wasn't afraid of them. Viki, downstairs? Cynthia?

The door to the study was ajar and light streamed from it. Lucy went down, pushed the door open, and went in. Cynthia was sitting on the edge of the leather couch, a glass in her hand. Her red hair was disordered, her face drawn. She looked up and almost dropped the glass.

"I'm sorry if I woke you, Mother," she said. "I couldn't sleep."

Lucy looked at the glass. This wasn't like Cynthia; two drinks before dinner, the brandy, and now, at two in the morning . . . . "Are you ill?" she asked sharply.

"No. I told you I couldn't sleep . . . . Sorry," she said again.

Lucy went to the desk and sat down in Sam's chair. It was worn; she wouldn't have had it any other way. It was, she'd often fancied, shaped to the contours of his big vital body. It had sturdy arms and a back you could lean against.

"You came up here to tell me something," she said after a moment.

"Yes, I guess so," Cynthia admitted dully, "then I thought better of it." Her hand shook; the ice tinkled, and liquid sloshed.

"Tell me now," Lucy said. She thought: Her defenses are down. "It's about Edward," she decided aloud.

Cynthia took a swallow; she had a little difficulty with it. She said after a moment, "Well, you'd know soon enough, I suppose. He's left me."

Lucy stiffened and her heart hammered for a moment, but she said evenly, "You've had quarrels before this."

"He left me," said Cynthia, not listening, "nine years ago."

"You never said——"

"You were away; father had died . . . no, I didn't tell anyone, but Viki remembers it."

"She knows about this too?"

"She couldn't help knowing. She could hear us shouting at each other," said Cynthia wearily. "Besides, I told her the next morning. It's a woman again."

"It was a woman the first time?"

"Of course. But that didn't last, he was home again in two weeks. And I forgave him," Cynthia said, her voice rising.

"Hush," said Lucy. "You don't want Viki to hear."

"Who cares? This time he says it's serious. He wants a divorce."

Lucy felt astonishment, dismay, and some compassion. She said, "Dearie, he probably doesn't; not really."

"What am I supposed to do? Sit and wait until he changes his mind?"

"I'd do just that if I were you."

"How do you know what you'd do?" Cynthia demanded. "You've not been through this, once, twice, or maybe in between without knowing it. Father never looked at another woman."

Lucy laughed, and Cynthia winced as if she'd been struck.

"Your father was a man, Cynthia," Lucy said, "and all of him was alive. Of course he looked at other women; he liked them; he admired them; he was charming with them. The important fact is that all he did was look. He was," she added slowly, "a happy man; happy—with me."

Cynthia said roughly, "And Edward's never been. Is that what you're driving at?"

"I don't know. I've never been in your confidence."

"Edward talks to you."

"Of course; we like each other. I'm fond of him and he, I think, is fond of me."

Cynthia said, "I might have known you'd take his part!"

"I'm not taking anyone's part. If you were to ask me to advise you, I'd say ride the storm out . . . and, if given time, it doesn't subside, then divorce him."

"I won't," Cynthia said, sullen. "I've given him no cause, none whatsoever."

"Spare me 'the best years of my life' routine, Cynthia."

"Well, haven't they been?"

"Oh, I know. You kept his house, slept with him, bore his children. Perhaps it wasn't enough."

"What more is there?"

"A great deal."

Cynthia said abruptly, "You've never really liked me, have you?"

Lucy was silent. Then she said, "No, not very much. But I loved you. Whether that's purely biological or not I don't know."

"Jack," said Cynthia, "always Jack. Because he was like father, and because he died."

"No to the last conclusion," said her mother sharply. "Yes, I suppose, to the first."

"As to that," said Cynthia, emptying her glass, her

speech a little slurred, "I've never really liked you. I was proud of you, admired you. I wanted to be like you, but I wasn't. I don't know who I'm like."

"Your father's mother," said Lucy. "She scared me too."

Cynthia looked at her, wholly astonished. "You mean, I scare you?"

"Oh, yes," Lucy told her. "Even when you were little. So self-possessed, so—forgive me—self-satisfied. Your father thought it amusing. I didn't."

"Father understood me."

"On the contrary," Lucy said. "And he always had a blind spot about his mother."

"I don't remember her," Cynthia said.

"You would have gotten along very well. You look like her, Cynthia. You are even handsomer, and she was a very attractive woman."

She rose, and Cynthia stood up, and walked somewhat unsteadily toward the bar.

"No," said Lucy, "you're going to bed. I'll give you a sleeping pill."

"I have some. . . . I just thought . . . a nightcap——"

"You aren't used to nightcaps," said her mother. "We'll talk tomorrow."

Cynthia said, "I don't suppose we've really said anything. When I think of Edward . . ." Her voice shook. "Cheap," she said. "Disgusting, a man of his age."

"He isn't old."

"Sex," said Cynthia violently.

"I daresay," Lucy said. "And if it's sex without love, he'll come back. . . . But if it's love with sex, then possibly he won't." Poor Edward, she thought.

Cynthia said, "He'll have to support me and the girls as well as that woman."

"Perhaps she can support herself; and perhaps he will come to the conclusion that he can't afford two women; business isn't good. My income from the mills is smaller; yours too. Edward's must have dropped considerably."

"Mother. . . ."

Lucy put her arms around her daughter, felt her trembling. Looking down from her slight advantage in height at the red head, she said after a moment, "There, dearie, let me put you to bed," and thought of how many times she'd said those words to a small Cynthia, hurt or angry, with her curious self-possession gone for a vulnerable moment.

Later, standing by one of the guest-room beds, she had watched Cynthia take the sleeping tablet; she had sat beside her until the shaking and the occasional whimpering stopped. She had said, "Don't come down to breakfast; Reba will bring it to you. Try to sleep."

And Cynthia had said with stark simplicity, "I feel awful."

"Of course." Lucy leaned down to kiss the damp cheek and thought: And worse tomorrow. "Just sleep," she said. "And call me if you need me."

Back in her own bed she thought: She needed me tonight and I, of course, failed her. Her father wouldn't have. He would have said the right thing, and been furious at Edward, which is what Cynthia wants of me. And Sam wouldn't have thought about their relationship—his daughter's and Edward's. He wouldn't have wanted to think about it because she was his daughter.

By that time there was a faint cold light on the eastern horizon, and Lucy lay watching it. She doubted she'd feel up to a breakfast herself, but she'd get up, pour coffee, and talk to Viki and Reba.

You really can't get anywhere with your children, she thought. Perhaps I couldn't have with Jack if he'd lived.

 5

Driving to Peaceable, Paul McDonald thought about New England's changing landscape. It had everything going for it—if you overlooked a whimsical climate—ocean, rivers, lakes, ponds, the Sound, salt marshes, meadows, mountains, and small villages. It had rocks and hills and an awareness of pioneers clawing a living from the hostile soil. He also thought about poverty, pollution, endangered wild life, murdered trees.

The Woods Hole experience—studying the pollution of the tides—had been exciting, absorbing and frightening, and the first of next month he'd be learning more in the new science center in Boston. Viki would be somewhere in the city; he would be with her whenever possible. They'd both be occupied, but it would be basically their last really free time. He thought of her long heavy hair, the curve of her cheek and breast, the way her eyes shone or clouded, the way she laughed, or sobered, looking at him with touching gravity. A line from Tennessee Williams—from "Summer and Smoke" wasn't it?—drifted into his mind: "This affliction of love." But it was not yet an affliction; it could become so. Whether it was love or not he did not know—the wanting to be near her, to hold her; wanting to listen and talk, or to fall silent; wanting to question, explore, and discover.

Viki was not his first experience. When he had been seventeen and in high school, there had been a girl—older and knowledgeable in her field. In school she was not exactly stupid, simply uninterested. All she wanted was to get passing marks. Her only school enthusiasm had been the football team of which Mac was a member.

She had shabby, careless parents who went out a lot as did her siblings—she was the youngest and left to her own devices. Sometimes he remembered with distaste and a curious sense of gratitude the evenings in the cluttered, not very clean parlor, or upstairs in the equally untidy bedroom she shared with a sister. Her mother and father usually returned late, and he'd be gone. "Better be on your way, big boy," she'd say. He'd encountered them only twice and they had been friendly to him, as probably they were to other gentlemen callers. "How about a beer?" her paunchy, sweating male parent had asked genially on both occasions.

She hadn't even been a pretty girl, but then, with her undeniable gifts, she hadn't needed to be. Later he heard that she'd married before graduation.

There had been other short-lived, quite different episodes. Two, to be exact, both casual, while he'd been working as usual during the summers. The last one had been the summer after his freshman year.

One girl had been holidaying with another office worker on the Cape; the other, older than Mac, had been waiting on tables in the resort motel in the mountains where he had also been employed.

It was afternoon when he pulled off the main road to follow an EAT sign along a blacktop; there was very little traffic, no stinking trucks roared past; there were trees here, and he saw farms, silos rising, and cows in the pastures. It was hot and the small, clean place wasn't air-conditioned, but there was a big floor fan. Mac sat at a counter stool and the wiry man behind the counter said, "Hi. Nice day, ain't it? . . . What'll you have?"

Mac considered the blackboard menu, his appetite leaning toward a sandwich and a Coke, or if they had it—yes, they did—a frosted, or a milk shake. He thought a moment and then said, "Hamburger, rare, and black coffee."

"Massachusetts?" inquired the counterman.

"That's right," Mac admitted. He thought, with longing, of a cold drink, and then shook his head. He had to watch his weight. Why he was inclined to put it on, he didn't know. He ate lightly, at home, and in college; he did push-ups. Regular exercise was not on his schedule, just hiking and considerable walking. But when he and Viki had a snack or a meal . . . well, pizzas didn't help, he supposed—nor did sandwiches. They went dutch except on the few occasions when he said, "I've saved a couple of bucks," and she permitted him to pay the check.

Certainly he hadn't—as far as he knew—inherited his inclination toward extra pounds from his parents. His mother was a little woman, always actively steaming around, herding her children, cooking, scrubbing; she had never weighed over a hundred and five pounds. The father, a bookkeeper in a small mercantile establishment, was almost as tall as Mac but a splinter of a man, not an additional ounce. He was of Scottish descent; his wife, of English ancestry, now lost in the past, for her family had lived in the Commonwealth since before the Tea Party.

Must be metabolism, thought Mac gloomily. He'd been thin as a boy, playing baseball, football, cutting lawns, working in stock rooms, heaving big cartons around. Before high school, whatever free time he'd had on long summer evenings had been spent in sandlot sports with other kids his age.

"Going far?" asked the counterman.

"Place called Peaceable," Mac told him, smiling. He had an open engaging grin; the counterman warmed to him as most people did. He asked, "Your burger okay?"

"Fine."

"You coulda had some French fries."

Mac sighed. He had a thing for French fries, and for fish and chips. "I know, but my girl told me a while back I was getting fat," he said.

She'd said, "Mac, watch your diet or you'll wind up looking like Robert Morley or Orson Welles—not that I don't love them both dearly."

She should worry! Viki was willow slim; but she didn't often bend like a willow; usually she was an oak.

"Have a nice trip," said the counter man as Mac was leaving. "I've been to Peaceable a time or two; it's a nice town. Not much industry there, so it stays pretty clean. . . . Mainly there's the Pemberton textile mills—friend of mine took me through—quite a sight. A great many mills have moved south, of course, but this one has stayed put. Employs —or used to anyway—a lot of help and they live good; neat little cottages, garden plots. I remember I thought: Damned if I wouldn't like to work there. But I can't stand machinery. I don't even like cars, toasters, refrigerators, or this here grille. But I accept 'em."

Mac went out, laughing, and then thought. Pemberton Mills? He was going to Mrs. Samuel Pemberton's; he was on his way.

Walking around his car, he smote the hood an affectionate light blow. It was a small coupé, old, but in good condition. Mac didn't mind machinery; he liked it, and knew something about it. His father's main interest outside of his family and job was tinkering with old cars. He could have been a working mechanic and made a lot more money perhaps, but he came from a long line of professional people (the mercantile house was as close as it had ever come to trade)—editors, ministers, doctors, engineers. None of them ever got rich, but as far as Mac could learn, listening to his father's slow thoughtful recollections, they'd been happy.

Maybe it's the snacks, he thought, getting into the car. Half the time I don't eat three regular meals. He saw himself as a boy running on a public beach, chasing gulls, or skipping flat rocks; he saw himself barreling around the sandlots, hollering—all kids hollered—or on a baseball diamond or a football field, burning up his energy. Study burned it up too, but he hadn't grown thin on studying. Driving along what eventually became a winding country road, he remembered his first bike. He'd worked for that. . . .

Metabolism? Physiology was an interesting subject, and biology another. His minor was biology. Heredity was mysterious and exciting: from his mother his coloring; from his father the early interest in books; from the one grandfather he'd known, an awareness of right and wrong with which he still struggled. Evaluations had changed since Grandpa McDonald, from his pulpit in the little church, thundered at his small devoted congregation. He'd been, early, a widower, had not remarried, and had died when Mac was thirteen. He had never known that grandmother, and only vaguely remembered his maternal grandfather; better, of course, his mother's mother who had left him the locket.

He thought: We don't seem to be blessed—if it is a blessing—with longevity.

Now, at nearly the end of his journey, he began to feel uneasy, almost ill. It hadn't been the hamburger, which was a good one; nor was it the strong black coffee. No. It was just the physical feeling which sometimes attacked him when he was uptight. What the hell was he uptight about? Meeting his girl's grandmother? Nuts to that. Old women liked him. He was not an innocent. He was aware that he'd been given considerable charm, but he rarely used it consciously. Seeing Viki's mother again? He'd met her just that once—and for a few minutes—but he'd formed a definite impression of her—Cynthia was an impressive woman—handsome, unflappable, and cold, Mac had thought; efficient, pleasant, chilly. He gravitated naturally toward warmth, having himself a reservoir of it and, driving back to the city with his cousin, he had thought carelessly of Edward Warren: Poor guy.

That was all surface stuff. What did Paul McDonald know about Warren or his wife? Could be the other way around. Maybe she was unflappable because she had to be. Perhaps she was a passionately loving wife. Perhaps the shoe was on the masculine foot and Edward was too grabbed by whatever it was he did in the advertising racket to feel anything but fatigue and possibly indifference toward Viki's mother?

Who knew anyone? Did he really know Viki? Yes, of course; but only in relation to himself.

It struck him, suddenly and sharply, like an unexpected slap in the face, that what he was feeling now, this minute, on a sunny afternoon in June in New Hampshire, could very well be guilt.

Hell! Who felt guilty in this era? If you did, you paid good money to lie on a couch and tell the shrink everything you'd done or thought since—or even before—the playpen, so that he would tell you what you felt guilty about. Hadn't Mac felt guilty that evening in Westchester? Too many people, too much laughter and noise, a big display of decorations, and the great tree. Somehow his Presbyterian grandfather had kept reminding him it was all not only superfluous expense but a holdover from paganism. He'd talked very little with Viki, and hardly at all with her parents. He couldn't somehow connect her with them in his mind.

This was different . . . going to her grandmother's, staying there until tomorrow. Somehow he'd manage to tell Viki that they had to play it cool, that discretion was the better part of—what? Decency? He hadn't minded—certainly not at the time—making out with the girl in the shabby, undusted, unmopped house, or encountering her parents. He had felt only excitement and a rather smug sense of having escaped the wrath, not of God, but of her loose-bellied, slightly repulsive father. If the old man had been upset, he might just have said, "You two get yourselves to a judge or someone fast or I'll see your folks, Mac. He had not felt guilty in the presence of her mother, a still pretty slattern who talked incessantly. The only sense of guilt he'd experienced was toward his own parents and he thanked heaven that they had not known about, much less met, the girl.

Eventually, following Viki's directions, he came to a gas station, stopped his car, and when a man emerged, asked, "Dan?"

"That's right. . . . You Viki's friend Mac?"

Mac nodded. He said, "I'd better have gas for the trip back. Fill her up will you, Dan? And I'd like to wash up."

Dan gave him the key. "Help yourself," he said, and looked after his customer with approval. Big kid, friendly. He'd give him the right directions, he told himself, smiling.

He said, when Mac came back to the car, "I've got a boy just finished his freshman year at Blue Mountain. You go there, don't you?"

"Yes, Viki and I are in the same class. What's your boy's name?"

"Dan Burton, Jr."

"I'll look for him next year."

"We thought there wouldn't be a next year," said

young Dan's father. "He had a sort of uphill road with the marks. Okay now. He's a tough kid; wants to make the football team. Bet you did."

"Oh," said Mac, laughing. "My nose? That was broken in high school the first time. I haven't had time at Blue Mountain for football."

"First time? Was there a second?"

"That was a fight," said Mac gravely. "Not my fight. I just sort of stepped in between a couple of guys, trying to break it up. They broke me up instead."

"On you it looks good," Dan told him. "Yep. Listenin' to radio and TV and readin' the papers makes you think more and more that this is no time to get involved in someone else's scrap. I dunno how you feel about this lousy war. I was in Korea. So okay. But I'm damned if I want Dan, Jr.——" He broke off, and added, "Well, Viki will be looking for you. I'll call her and tell her you're on your way."

"Thanks, Dan. . . . How about directions?"

Dan gave them to him, and Mac listened with part of his mind. The rest was running along country roads and up a hill and into an unknown house.

"Have a good stay," said Dan. "Come back soon." He thought, watching the little car leave the station: Bet Viki'll be glad to see him.

6

CYNTHIA, WHO HAD NOT APPEARED for breakfast, managed to come down for lunch. Twice Lucy had looked in on her to ask briskly, "Are you all right?" and twice she'd answered, "Yes, just a slight headache." But the second time had added, "I don't suppose you're surprised," and Lucy had agreed, "No . . . try to rest. . . . Viki's young man is coming. Remember?" At which Cynthia had moaned faintly and turned on her side away from the open windows, although the shades were pulled down.

The last thing Cynthia wanted was to make small talk with one of Viki's boy friends. Reba had brought up her breakfast, saying, "Your mother says you're not feeling up to snuff," to which Cynthia had agreed wanly. Then, supplied with a backrest from the closet shelf, she had surveyed her tray with a brief shudder. However, Lucy had overseen it; a lot of black coffee, sugar to be used if desired, unbuttered toast, and tomato juice.

"You just set the tray down outside the door if you're up to it," Reba suggested, "or on the floor if you'd rather. There's nothing to spoil. I hope you feel better, Cyn." Reba was the only one—except years ago, Edward—who had ever called her that; well, today she felt like it.

Cynthia ate a piece of toast and drank two cups of coffee. She'd thought an hour or so earlier, crawling out of bed to go to the bathroom: I have a hangover. She'd never had the experience before; yet, she argued, returning to bed, it isn't only that. Not even two drinks on an empty stomach plus the brandy, and then, much later, another drink in one equally empty. No. It's also the tension and anxiety and humiliation.

She had wished not to encounter her mother today, although there was no escape. But the first time Lucy had knocked and come in, on the heels of a whispered permission, she'd been so matter of fact, almost casual . . . perhaps nothing more would be said. Cynthia could not remember fully all that had been said at two in the morning; she recalled some of the short dialogue centering about herself and Jack, and the not-liking. She'd never mention it again; she hoped Lucy wouldn't. But hadn't her mother said, "We'll talk tomorrow?"

What was there to discuss further.

SHORTLY AFTER NOON, having slept a little, Cynthia felt a little better physically. She carried the tray carefully, for she was pretty shaky, and set it down outside her door. Bending made her slightly dizzy, but she was afraid to take it downstairs with the juice untouched.

There were sounds from below: a vacuum cleaner, Reba's voice, a door shutting, other voices drifting in from outside, and laughter. Lucy and Viki? They were great friends.

Bathing, dressing in pale blue slacks and a navy shirt, getting her navy cardigan from the bureau drawer, doing her hair, creaming her face, putting on a little foundation—

I look like death, she thought—Cynthia was remembering a little more; her mother's advice, for instance.

She hadn't asked for it—or had she?—and she wouldn't take it. She was a grown woman; she would make her own decisions. She had already made the important one. Edward could wait until hell froze over for his divorce; if he tried to free himself, she'd fight him in court. She wouldn't give him or the woman—what was her name? He had said it a time or two—Lisa, that was it; just Lisa.

He'd have to explain the situation to the girls; she wouldn't. And if, given time, as her mother had suggested, he did come back, asking pardon or at least amnesty . . . ? She'd see when the time came. She wouldn't change; there was no reason for her to change; if there were any changing, he'd have to do it.

At lunch, Cynthia could eat a little: the fresh salad, the cold chicken, and tea. "Could I have it hot instead of iced?" she asked Reba, and Lucy said approvingly, "Now, you'll feel better," and Viki asked, "One of your migraines, Mom?"

Cynthia had had migraine headaches occasionally ever since she was a young girl. Twice after her marriage she'd seen a doctor; she was tired of being laid up for two or three painful days—hurting, nauseated, lights shooting behind her closed lids. And the first doctor had said, "We don't know too much about this type of disorder, but we're working on it. Sometimes it's an allergy, though for a long time people thought it a form of indigestion. Nowadays, one of the theories is that it's tension; another, purely psychological."

He'd given her medicine which cured the headaches but made her more nauseous and after a while she learned to live with the condition, as the second doctor had suggested, and to find her own remedy. He'd had still another theory;

a sudden drop in blood sugar. So she took to her bed as usual, rested, and when she could eat, started with something sweet.

Viki thought: Mom must have told Gran sometime last night. She had not been awake at two in the morning; she had slept, deeply, happily, her dreams filled with images of love.

Lucy thought: No use my starting it all over again. I wonder how much Cynthia remembers? Better let her make the next move—if any. I wish I could talk to Edward, but even if I could, it wouldn't do; it wouldn't do at all.

After lunch Cynthia went upstairs again, having walked awhile in the gardens at her mother's insistence. "Do you good," Lucy said. "Besides Reba will want time to put your room in order." So when Cynthia finally reached that once-familiar girlhood haven, the bed was made, the tray removed, and everything, as Reba put it, "neated up."

Cynthia lay down on the bed, careless for once of her freshly pressed slacks. She pulled the shades down again and did not bother to switch on the radio. She could hear music from downstairs—the stereo. But it did not disturb her. She had taken a mild tranquilizer, hoping to escape into sleep.

Viki and her grandmother were listening to the music. "How about your nap, Gran?" Viki asked.

"Later. Twenty minutes before dinner perhaps." Lucy smiled. She had for a great many years taken a brief nap when possible; sometimes before lunch, otherwise before dressing for dinner. Often Sam had come to lie beside her; sometimes he too slept; often he just lay there, watching her sleep; she could feel him watching, even in her light dreams; sometimes he woke her, and took her into his arms. She remembered Spain, especially Spain, when they were free, and absurdly happy. "It's marvelous," she'd commented. "Old people like us."

"Who's old?" he'd demanded.

Spain had been a peak, a culmination, a reward perhaps, for working as hard as Sam had worked, or for the anxious long years of the Depression, or for bringing up their children. A reward possibly for rising above, if never completely outgrowing, their grief over Jack. Spain had offered a time to laugh, a time to dream, a time to plan the future.

Lucy and Viki were listening to the Irish Rovers LP. "That unicorn song!" said Lucy. "How ever did you remember?"

"I know you by heart," said Viki, laughing. "Want to hear the Carpenters after?"

"Yes."

Later, after the stereo had been turned off, she remarked, "You're a nice child, Viki, and you can hardly sit still waiting for—what's his name?"

"Mac, to you."

"Mac, then."

"I'm sitting perfectly still," argued Viki indignantly. "I'm not tossing my hair, or clawing my scalp—you don't like it—I'm not even tapping my foot."

"Your heart is dancing."

"Okay. Aren't you going to ask me, 'Is this serious?' "

"No. I doubt you've quite made up your mind. Sometimes the heart runs ahead of the mind. What's he like, your Mac?"

"He isn't my Mac really. No one belongs to anyone else."

"Don't generalize. I admit that 'belonging' is rare. So what's he like?"

"Oh—big, and mostly gentle, great fun, and very serious."

"About you?"

"No. About life, and work, and what's going on now, and what's going to happen. You'll have to draw your own conclusions about him, Gran. At the moment anyhow, I think he's Something Else!"

"It's a good thing that I occasionally read contemporary novels and current magazines," said Lucy austerely, "or I wouldn't understand you. I often think I'll never do it again, but one does pick up a little of today's argot—which apparently changes from month to month."

"Right on," said Viki. "What bothers you about magazines and novels? The words, the phrases?"

Lucy said, "They don't shock me if that's what you mean, but they revolt me."

Viki said, "Well, sometimes, me too." She added, after a moment, "I may as well tell you now that Mom and Dad have had a terrific row. I couldn't help hearing, so she had to tell me . . . Was it yesterday morning?" she wondered aloud.

"I know. Your mother told me very early this morning, or if you prefer, late last night."

"I thought so. Gran, she swears it's Splitsville!"

Lucy sighed. "Yes—as you phrase it—for the moment——"

"What are you going to do about it, Gran?"

Lucy looked astonished. "I? Nothing. This is between your parents. Oh . . . advise, you mean? I've lived long enough to realize that no one wants advice even if they ask for it—unless, of course, it concurs with what they already intend to do; but if it runs counter, forget it." Lucy shrugged; then added, "Your grandfather and I differed, now and then; sometimes we even quarreled. We weren't exactly Darby and Joan."

"Who?"

"Never mind. Look it up. Sam and I were two people; we had opinions; we were often selfish; we had healthy egos. Each of us was subject to irritations, anger, frustration; rarely, as it happened, at the same time, which was very good. But we never went to bed mad. Your uncle Jack used to say that, when he was little, after being punished: "I'm not going to bed mad." It's a good thing to remember. No doubt your generation would call it corny, if the word's still in use. St. Paul said it, perhaps in a more general connection, 'Let not the sun go down upon your wrath.' King James version," she remarked parenthetically.

Viki laughed. She said, "You're the most. Do you still go to church, Gran?"

"Why, yes, though not as often as once I did. I'm sorry to say I don't much like the new minister . . . well, he's been here five years actually. Of course I'm away winters. There's a church I like near my hotel in Florida. As for Peaceable, I still miss Doctor Grant. But you wouldn't remember him." She rose and walked across to Viki's chair. She said, "Try not to fret, Viki," and stroked her granddaughter's shining hair.

"I do, of course," Viki admitted; "and Jenny will be devastated when she finds out."

"No one goes scot free on this earth," her grandmother said, "although sometimes it seems so. Most parents try to shield their children from suffering—physical, mental, and emotional. Often, they can't. Sometimes they won't. Every generation proclaims that each must lead his own life, but seldom grants the subsequent generation the right to lead theirs."

The telephone rang there in the study and Viki reached it in one fluid motion. She said, "Who? . . . Oh Dan. . . . He is? . . . Thanks; you're a doll."

She turned from the instrument and reported, "Mac stopped at Dan's to ask directions, so he'll be here any minute."

"Go out and meet him," suggested Lucy. "Sit on a stone wall and—as you so gracefully put it—claw your scalp. Go fly a kite or chase a squirrel. I'll hover around until I've given him the official elderly welcome."

Viki gave her a rib-crushing hug, "Don't peek out the window," she advised. "Be sedate; stay in the living room with your pretty ankles crossed and your hands folded in your lap. Leave us burst upon you like a couple of brand-new stars."

Smiling, Lucy went into the living room, did exactly as bidden, and waited, thinking: I used to run to meet Sam when he came to see me at home, at Aunt Gwen's—or anywhere—even when his home became my home and it was office quitting time. She thought gravely: Actually I'm running to meet him now, to keep an appointment; when or where I don't know, but whenever and wherever, that will be home.

Viki went no farther than the rose garden where she would be able to hear the car before she saw it. She walked— not hurrying physically—stooping her young face to an open rose, closing her eyes, feeling the sun, smelling the fragrence.

There . . . ! She flew around the corner of the house and onto the driveway.

Mac's little car swerved, pulled up, and stopped. He put his head out of the window and howled, "You lost your marbles or something? I could have run over you."

"Not me," Viki told him. "I know when to get out of the way. Hi!"

"Hi," said Mac as he opened the car door, got out, and took her in his arms. And they said simultaneously, "I've missed you."

He'd forgotten his own instructions to himself. Kissing tends to bring on woolgathering, even amnesia.

"Hey," he said presently. "I promised myself, no public display of affection . . . perhaps not even in private—here."

"No one's around. The staff—consisting of my grandfather's cousin, Reba, and the current cook—are somewhere dreaming up dinner; Mom's lying down, Gran is waiting for us inside; she'll wait another minute. Leave the car there, mine's in the garage, we might take a drive after supper; first come and look at the roses; the light on them is fantastic."

They strolled into the rose garden, which Cynthia could see from her windows. Having heard the car, she got up and peeked out. She could see Mac's back only, his bent head, and Viki's arms about him. . . . Of course, everybody kissed everybody nowadays; it had been going on for a long time. Your male guests kissed you; your female guests kissed your husband; and boys and girls had kissed each other, probably since Adam. But Cynthia Warren knew a casual kiss when she experienced or saw one, and she turned from the window, frowning. Viki is very like Edward, she thought, and she'd certainly been kissed before—kisses as ordinary as a handshake. But, one day . . . perhaps right now . . . ?

She heard Viki laugh, and then the footsteps going back around the house, to the front door. She thought: Mother will probably think he's a delightful young man. She's always liked men.

"Hi," said Viki from the hallway. "You in the living room, Gran?"

"You told me to be," Lucy answered.

They went in and Viki said, "Gran, this is Mac."

Lucy rose to offer her hand. "So it is," she agreed, smiling.

"And, probably in your honor, he's gone formal," Viki said, and Lucy lifted an eyebrow. Slacks, a shirt with an open collar, moccasins. . . ?

"Well, it's formal for Mac," Viki explained. "I'll show him his room."

"I've a flight bag in the car," Mac said, "and a sweater. Not that I do any flying," he told Lucy. You can buy them anywhere."

"Take him upstairs; then come back. Mac can find his way down again, I think. Your mother will join us for a drink. . . . We have an unfashionably early supper hour," she told Mac. "Viki's grandfather preferred it. Except, of course, when we were in Spain—it took us awhile to get used to eating there in practically the middle of the night."

"I've always wanted to go to Spain, Mrs. Pemberton."

"Then go," she advised. "Don't miss it." She thought; Will you ever go, and will you take Viki with you?

Out to the car, back with the bag and sweater, and up to Mac's quarters. They were circumspect, Viki aware that her mother's door could open at any moment. She said, "Here it is, and your own bathroom; my grandfather had a Thing about bathrooms—they're all over the place. This was Uncle Jack's room," she added, "my mother's brother. I never knew him. He was killed in the Second World War. . . . 'Bye. See you downstairs at the bar. You'd rather have beer, wouldn't you?"

"Anything."

"I'll check," and she went off, smiling, to report to Lucy, "Mac likes beer best."

And Lucy said indulgently, "There should be some on ice. Reba likes it too."

Presently they were all assembled. Cynthia came

downstairs, still in her pale blue slacks and navy shirt, but she'd pampered her face and brushed her pretty hair. Viki was still wearing the multicolored full short skirt and mexican blouse she'd worn at lunch. Her makeup was, as usual, eye shadow—she didn't need mascara—and lipstick.

Cynthia thought: Well, she didn't dress up for him; maybe that's a good sign. But you couldn't tell these days. When Jenny wanted to impress a boy, for instance, she meticulously looked like something out of the ragbag. Cynthia would complain, "How can you get yourself up like that?" and Jenny, wounded, would respond, "It's the fun way, and besides I like it."

There was a camp shop in the far end of town, modeled on similar places in the city. Jenny would spend her ample allowance on costumes from the twenties or thirties, and bits and pieces of curious trappings—in which she looked, always, young, absurd, and delightful.

"You remember Mac, Mom?" Viki was saying.

They shook hands and Cynthia replied, "Of course."

He said he was glad to see her again, and Lucy asked briskly, "What's everyone drinking?"

Reba came in with a couple of bottles of beer. More introductions . . . and Reba regarded Mac thoughtfully. She was, she assured herself, too sensible to worry about Viki, who would have half a dozen or more young men around before she settled down.

Sherry for Lucy, beer for Mac and Reba, dry vermouth on the rocks for Viki, but Cynthia said, "I'd like tomato juice. . . . No, Reba, just straight," she added in answer to Reba's "With vodka?"

"That's good," said Reba. "You didn't drink your juice this morning."

There was a pleasant, seemingly relaxed half hour or more, before supper. Viki, both amused and irritated, listened to Cynthia's courteous probing. Mac lived in Boston? She adored Boston. She knew a great many people there.

Mac said, well he didn't really; only those in his neighborhood, people who'd gone to school with him, and his parents' friends. He'd been away a lot, working summers from the time he was sixteen; and once for an entire year, before entering college—traveling around, getting jobs when and where he could.

Cynthia said quite sincerely that this was very commendable, and asked what he was majoring in and thought that was commendable too. Their town, she explained, like practically every other, was greatly disturbed about environmental conditions. She was on several committees, she told him.

At supper Lucy and Viki made most of the conversation. Reba listened, occasionally disappearing into the kitchen. Mac listened, and Cynthia pretended to, but did not—which was apparent to everyone at the table, including young Mr. McDonald. She simply isn't with it, he concluded, and wondered what was on her mind. Me? he inquired of himself. No, he decided. He doubted that Mrs. Warren would consider him a menace.

Actually she *was* thinking about him. He disturbed her. He had an almost tangible vitality, which didn't express itself in words or gestures; it was just there, like the quiescent fire in a volcano. Masculine, Cynthia concluded, and added to herself, while smiling brilliantly at their guest, the animal type. It was most distasteful to her; Edward had it, in abundance.

After supper, they drifted into the study and Mac, looking at the portrait over the mantel, asked, "Viki's grandfather?"

Lucy nodded and he said, "She looks a little like him, doesn't she?"

"Oh yes, although most people don't see it. Her coloring and her eyes are like her father's. But there's a way she moves her head—though that doesn't show in a portrait—and something about the forehead and mouth."

Viki expostulated, "You sound as if you were talking about a show dog's ancestry."

"Champions," said Lucy.

They listened to the news, most of it bad: unemployment in the state, local unrest, a murder not far away; unemployment in the nation, strikes, riots! Trouble in London, Paris, Rome, Tokyo . . . and always, of course, the war.

"Let's have some music," Lucy suggested, and Viki sat across the room from Mac, listening as he discussed pop and classical music, rock, jazz, and blues with her grandmother.

Lucy said firmly, "Mark my word, jazz is coming back; also the old songs. The blues are already with us; rock's fading. . . . You wait and see." She added, "Shut the radio off for a minute, Viki, I want to ask Mac something. . . . What do you think of the quasi-religious-oriented music?"

"The Jesus turn-on?" he asked.

Cynthia twitched her shoulders. "I don't much like the term," she commented.

"I don't either," said Lucy, "but it's current. And the interest in it is growing. Some of it seems pretty commercial to me."

Mac shrugged, and said, "I suppose many of my generation are looking for something to hold on to. This is considerably better than some of the other turn-ons—and if they find something—like hope, for instance—I think it doesn't much matter what the angle or the pitch is."

Lucy said, "I'm still of my generation. I like the old spirituals. . . . You ever heard Marian Anderson, Mac?"

"Just recordings; she's great."

"And the old hymns; doleful, some of them, and I

suppose you'd say corny. But there are still some very comforting hymns, quite lovely."

Mac said, "I was brought up on them to some extent. I like them too, Mrs. Pemberton."

They talked about Mahalia Jackson and Odetta; about the old orchestra band music, now popular again; country Western, and the dozens of singers—Sinatra, Tony Bennett, and those who had been and were no more, Billie Holiday, and others, until Cynthia, bored and impatient, rose and said, "If you'll excuse me, everyone, I still have a trace of a headache. See you tomorrow. . . . I hope you sleep well," she told Mac and something of her chilly charm came through.

"Mom's not very interested in the things we listen to," Viki apologized when she had left. "She's mad for opera, and she likes some of the melodic pop stuff but mostly symphonies, concertos." She laughed. "Sometimes Dad and I would sneak off to the playroom and have a ball, with the doors closed. Gran digs most of it and even if she doesn't, she listens."

"I've been alone a good deal for ten years," said Lucy. "Can't read all the time; can't garden at night. I detest long phone calls, and I don't have a great many people in, or go out. A little charity work, a board meeting, a tea party, a rubber of contract." She shrugged. "Besides, I like to have the radio on when I'm falling asleep, no matter where I am."

"Did Grandfather?" asked Viki.

"Heavens, no. He inclined, as your mother does, to the orthodox. 'As long as it has a tune,' he'd say. His idea of fun music was a rousing polka. I went along with him. But as I have to live in this world, it seems to me I'd better know what's going on, whether I like it or not."

"Gran," asked Viki, "would it be all right if Mac and I went for a drive in his car? It's still light."

She loved daylight saving, the slanting gold, the look of the sky, trees and flowers, the drowsy birds toward dusk.

"It won't be when you get back. . . . Reba——Where is she?"

"She said good night and left us before Mom did."

"I'm definitely getting senile," said Lucy, sighing. "I don't remember. But then she's always in and out like a shadow—a very quiet woman. She doesn't really like any kind of music. Says some of it's a pleasant noise, but most isn't. I'll lock up." She rose, fished in the desk drawer and gave Mac a key. "Viki would lose it," she predicted.

"I didn't know you ever locked up here," said Viki.

"We never did until the last few years, but even Peaceable has its problems. There was a strike at the mill last winter, for instance. I had to fly back from Florida for a few days. . . . Get a sweater, Viki. You too, Mac. It turns cool at night in June."

She saw them out, closed and locked the door, and went slowly up the stairs.

On the landing she was met by Satan, Reba's enormous black cat. He lived in the kitchen, in Reba's bedroom, and the small living room next to it, sometimes condescending to call on Sadie. Now and then, to Reba's dismay, he escaped to examine the rest of the house. "How do I know you wouldn't have some one visiting who's allergic to cats?" she'd say. But she'd always had a cat before she came to live here and during all of her Peaceable years.

Satan rubbed against Lucy's legs and purred. He had a loud friendly purr and Lucy stroked him, saying, "Better get back to Reba or she'll have your whiskers. On a night like this you should be outdoors, like some good witch's familiar. Ah well . . . since Reba took you to the vet, I suppose you can only supervise cat amusements. Poor thing!"

She went into her bedroom, thinking how much she still missed Shamrock, who had been Sam's mostly. The dog had died nine years ago, and she had not replaced him.

As Viki and Mac drove away, he said thoughtfully, "I think I'm in love with your grandmother."

"So is almost everyone who knows her—old, young, boy, girl. God knows why. She isn't beautiful—just handsome —and she's not brilliant. I've heard my mother say of her, 'I don't know what it is, but she always gets her own way without seeming to.'"

"Warmth," Mac diagnosed. "Interest in other people, Charm. . . . Do you remember your grandfather?"

"Of course. I was practically adult when he died—ten years ago. Jenny remembers him too. He was wonderful and he always had time for us when we came here or he visited us. I miss him."

"I miss you," said Mac. "Where do I turn? Where are we going?"

"I'll tell you."

"In time, please. Most females scream, 'Turn left' just as you're halfway past the road or exit, and generally because they're talking."

She gave him time to turn, before they reached the village. She said, "There's a special park, complete with planting, a small pool, lots of trees and trails. Grandfather owned the property; he gave it to the town."

"Can everybody use it?"

"Yes. It was sort of planned for the mill people and their kids; the company picnics are always held there, but anyone uses it who wants to. There's a sort of custodian evenings, and the men at the mill volunteer to keep the grounds picked up, cut the grass and water it. Gramp said if they feel the place belongs to them, they'll take care of it. It closes at midnight."

When they reached the spot, and drove in, the gates stood open; there was ample parking space. "Let's walk," Viki suggested. So they got out and Mac looked around him. The park was lighted but not too brightly, and he asked uneasily, "Won't the custodian come creeping around with a flashlight?"

"Nope. He'll just see the car and know you're from out of town, and if he looks for us—well—he's known me practically since I was born."

"Ever bring anyone else here?"

"Not recently, Officer. I've come with Gramp and with my father, of course; Gran too. We had family picnics here, came to the employees' bash. . . . Why?"

"I suppose it's called Pemberton Park?"

"People just call it 'The Park.' There are two others in Peaceable, as well as the Village Green, but somehow you always know which they mean."

They were now walking along a wide trail between trees where pine needles were fragrant and slippery beneath their feet. When they came to a clearing, it was round.

"Magic," said Viki. "My father used to tell me if we could come very late at night, very quietly, we'd see the elfin ring, and the little people dancing on toadstools. Let's sit here awhile."

They sat, a big tree at their backs, and Viki put her

sweater around her shoulders, but when Mac reached for her, it slipped off. He said, after a while, "I guess you're right— it is magic. Scares me."

"Why?"

" I didn't mean to fall in love for years."

She said, "That scares me too, but I like it."

He said, "About Boston, Viki . . ."

"What about it?"

"Have you told your family yet?"

"Not exactly. I shall. I'll tell Mom this weekend. She'll be upset."

"And your father?"

"He isn't home right now; I'll tell him when he returns, unless I've already left. In that case it will be up to her."

"Your mother doesn't like me," Mac told her.

"Well, it takes a while—getting to know her, I mean. Besides she has problems, just now."

He thought: Viki? No. Mr. Warren? But he did not ask questions. He was not a prying person. If Viki wanted to tell him anything, she would.

She didn't want to; it would be embarrassing, and besides she was loyal. Mac was, essentially, a stranger.

"Let's not talk," he said.

So they were silent, embracing in the dark lovely night, but after awhile she drew away, almost breathless, "No . . . we can't, Mac," she said.

"Okay." He leaned back against the tree and wished he hadn't quit smoking. "Well, about Boston . . . I'd like my family to meet you."

"Of course."

"Noisy kids," he said, "but my parents are sort of quiet. I think you'll like them."

"I hope they like me," she said. "What's really bugging you about Boston?"

78

"Well—all summer—of course, summers don't last, but I can't help thinking something might happen."

"It won't, but if it does, I suppose there are solutions. A little messy, but still solutions."

"Name one."

"Abortion."

"No!" he said violently.

"All right. . . . Then there's vanishing into some charitable refuge voluntarily, or being dragged away by one's parents—which I can't imagine—and returning flat, childless, and whispered about."

"Don't talk like that!"

"Also, of course, there's always suicide."

He shook her, and said, sharply, "Stop it. You don't have marriage on your emergency list, do you?"

"No. You don't want it; I don't want it. We'd be out of our skulls. You'd hate me after a while; maybe I'd hate you."

"No, I couldn't hate you."

"How do you know? . . . Mac, let's just have our summer, and after that"—she laughed—"who knows, you might turn up, unattached, at say, twenty-seven and still remembering me. I might even be unattached too. Climb a hill," she said dreamily, "and there's always another somewhere ahead. Turn one corner and wait for the next—for something unexpected, another view, another landscape."

"You're a funny kid, Viki."

"But you aren't laughing."

"No."

"I'm not funny. I'm just an ordinary chick, a little brighter than some, not as pretty as others. Passing grades."

Now he *was* laughing, and they collapsed into each other's arms for one of the mindless moments during which there is no past and no future. When they had sobered, she went on as if she'd never stopped. "Turning corners, sometimes you don't believe the next one will ever come, or the next hill; there's a plateau or something. The point is, keep on walking and be free!"

"You sound like Women's Lib."

"Oh, that! You ought to hear Gran on the subject."

"What's her opinion?"

"Just that she hasn't one, really. One time, when we were talking about it, she said she'd never felt un-liberated before—or after—she married. She was all for the girls getting equal pay and prestige or whatever, even if she thought some of their methods absurd. But she added that, as she had never had to earn her living, she's not in competition with men. Of course, she said, a woman's always in some sort of competition with other women, or with her children."

"She wasn't trained for anything?"

"Oh, sure. She was going to teach. But then she met Gramp. Really met him, I mean, like a head-on collision and seeing stars. Actually she'd known him since she was a kid. . . . Mac, it's time to go."

"What time is it?"

"I've no idea. An alarm went off in my head. It often does, and then I know it's time to move."

"And one went off a little while ago, I figure."

"That's right."

As they walked back along the trail, he asked, "Your grandmother won't be worried? I mean, about your being out with me?"

"No. She trusts me—unfortunately," said Viki sadly. "Not that I've ever asked her does she or doesn't she? . . . But, I know."

When they reached the parking space, the custodian was standing by Mac's car. He said, "I was just coming to find you, young feller. I'm closing up. . . . Well, I'll be darned! Viki!"

"Hi, Joe," she said, and they shook hands and beamed at each other in the parking-lot light. "This is Mac," she told him. "He's in my class at school."

"You staying with Mrs. P.?"

"Of course, both of us."

"Haven't seen you for a long time, Viki. You should come more often. Mrs. P. misses you. Tells me so when I run into her in town or to church, and now and then she comes here, evenings, before sundown or just after—sometimes alone, sometimes with folks from Boston or even New York and often of course with Miss Jones."

Reba was "Miss Jones," in Joe's book.

He waved them into the car and asked, "How's that little brat, Jenny?"

"Not as little, but still a brat. . . . 'Bye, Joe. Give my best to the family."

Joe said, "I'll wait on the lights till you're out of here." And Mac watched him limping across the parking lot.

Viki said, "Joe was in an accident at the mill. There was group insurance and Gramp saw to the rest; also—this was maybe fifteen years ago—he drew a pension . . . and now Social Security. So he and his wife still have their little house. Their children are grown, and his wife—one of the really indestructible people—gardens and sells vegetables and flowers. Joe helps. Now and then she comes to Gran's to lend a hand if there's a domestic crisis."

√"Can we just drive around a little?" asked Mac. "It's a fabulous night. Look at that moon."

The moon had risen late and hung suspended in the sky, in her last, luminous quarter.

"I don't see why not," said Viki, "but no parking," she added austerely, "and try to keep both hands on the wheel."

"Scrunch over," said Mac. "We'll both drive." He put his arm around her, and her hand on the wheel with his

81

over it. "Now give me directions—road directions, that is."

When finally and reluctantly they reached the house, a porch light burned, and one in the entrance hall, and another at the top of the staircase.

Mac hunted for the key. "If you've lost it," Viki whispered, "we'll go back to the car and I'll laugh myself to sleep. Far be it from me to ring."

He let himself in, and Viki followed. "Lock up," she went on, whispering. "I can turn out the lights from upstairs."

They went up quietly, handfast, and Viki said, "I'll walk you to your room, but do be quiet."

"Big feet," Mac murmured humbly.

He opened his door. Viki slid in and partly closed it. "You may kiss me good night," she said solemnly.

"I'm tired of kissing you," he said. "But I mustn't be rude."

She was laughing to herself when she slipped out and went down the hall. Her own door was only partly closed, and the light was on. Reba? I hope she's turned down the bed, Viki thought, yawning. That's my idea of luxury; bed turned down, night things laid out. She went in and stopped, startled, saying, "For Pete's sake! Is anything wrong, Mom?"

Cynthia was sitting in the big chair. She was smoking. She had stopped half a dozen times in the last three years. Yesterday, driving up to Peaceable, she had bought a pack of cigarettes at a gas station. Tonight, she had opened it; alone, she had started again.

"Surely, you aren't stupid," said Cynthia.

"You're smoking," Viki remarked. Literally and figuratively.

"Sit down. It's time we talked about your new friend."

Viki sat on the edge of her bed and Cynthia protested, from long habit, "Never sit on the edge of a bed; it's bad for the mattress."

"Okay." Viki shoved herself into the middle of the twin bed, sat up against the pillows, her feet under her, her hands clasped about her young knees. Cynthia regarded her with impersonal admiration: the long throat; the round chin; head well up; the brown, steady eyes so like Edward's.

"He isn't a new friend," Viki remarked. "We were freshmen together."

"But this"—Cynthia hesitated—"interest seems to be new."

"Not really." Viki laughed. "I've talked about him often. We've been going steady all the past year."

"What an idiotic expression. And how far have you gone?"

"You don't like Mac?"

"No."

"His hair's clean, and not as long as half our neighbors' boys."

"I'm accustomed to long-haired young men," said Cynthia. "I don't like your staying out half the night with him."

"I've stayed out, as you put it, half the night, with others."

"All of whom your father and I knew."

"Not all. I've been away. Remember? And I could tell you things about the ones you do know—all eligible, I suppose—which could make your hair curl. I haven't because I can take care of myself."

"I doubt it."

Viki said, exasperated, "All right. Lay it on the line. I asked Gran if it were all right to go for a drive in Mac's car."

"Your grandmother is indulgent when it suits her. Keep your voice down; she's next door. Answer me, Viki. How far have you gone?"

Viki said carefully, "Tonight, only as far as The Park."

"That's not what I meant, and you know it."

"Mac and I are guests here. It voluntarily restricts us. Now I guess it's time I told you that I have a job in Boston. I said something about it a while back, after I'd applied. I've had my interview and it's all set. I'm leaving on Friday. Also college approved. And an apartment with a classmate, Karen Banks."

"So?" said her mother. "I don't approve, nor will your father."

"When are you going to tell him?"

Cynthia flushed. She said, "There are ways of stopping you."

"Money? I have enough of my own to get along. Shot gun? It's hard to imagine Daddy using a gun except against defenseless birds."

"This is ridiculous," said her mother sharply. "Suppose you tell me the truth. Just what sort of relationship——?"

Viki interrupted. She said evenly, "Exactly what you're thinking, Mom."

"You can sit there and tell me——"

"Cool it," Viki advised. "Yes. And it's not exactly uncommon. I doubt that it ever was."

Cynthia rose. She was shaking; she would have said with shock. It wasn't. It was mainly anger. She thought: She's exactly like Edward.

She said so. She said, "You're very like your father."

"Can I help my genes?"

"Your grandmother . . ." Cynthia began and went to the connecting door.

Viki cried, "For heaven's sake let Gran sleep."

"You've listened to her when you wouldn't to me," Cynthia reminded her. "I'm leaving in the morning. I won't come down to breakfast."

84

Viki said, with her first touch of sullenness, "I couldn't care less. But you might think of Gran; she hates scenes."

But you don't, she thought. You love them. They give you a chance to throw things, cry, have migraines, look martyred.

Cynthia knocked at Lucy's door and Lucy said, "Come in, Cynthia."

"I begged you to keep your voice down," Cynthia told her daughter. Then she added, "Would you come here, Mother?"

They heard Lucy get out of bed. Cynthia opened the door, stood back and Lucy came in, barefoot and in her nightgown.

"You'll catch cold, Gran."

"No. . . . What is this all about? I heard you, of course."

"It's about Viki. I came in here to wait for her."

"I heard you. I hoped you'd get tired and go to bed, Cynthia."

Sometimes, Cynthia thought, her mother could be the most exasperating woman in the world. How had her father stood it?

She said, "Someone had to demand an explanation——"

"Of a drive. . . . Where'd you go, Viki?" Lucy asked, and sat down in the rocking chair. "The Park?"

"That's right." Viki slid off the bed, picked up the summer blanket at the foot of it and put it around her grandmother's shoulders.

"Thank you, dear," said Lucy. "Cynthia, why don't you go to bed? There's always tomorrow, or for some of us anyway."

Cynthia said harshly, "Will you stop talking trivia?

Viki has just admitted to me that she's had——" she stopped. "I looked out of this door and saw her coming out of that man's room," she added.

Viki said to her grandmother, "Not here, Gran. I just walked him there and went in for half a minute to say good night."

Lucy smiled. The child had scruples. She thought: She didn't get them from me!

"Sex!" said Cynthia with loathing. "Everything's sex —young, old, the ultimate pollution, in all the media, even from the so-called liberal pulpits—unrestricted, open, illicit. No matter how you try to bring up your children. . . . Not all parents are permissive," she added.

"Quite," agreed Lucy, regarding her daughter. "Viki's generation thinks it invented sex. Yours—if you're a valid example of it—wishes it never had been. I'm going to bed. Are you coming to church with me tomorrow, Cynthia?"

"I'm going home," Cynthia said shortly and went out, slamming the door.

"I'm sorry, Gran."

"No you're not. You're upset because the situation is now more or less in the open. I don't ask you to understand your mother, nor can she put herself in your place. I can only hope that you'll each be a little tolerant. That isn't exactly the word I want, but I'm too tired to hunt for another. Anyway, have sufficient comprehension to listen. Your mother's badly shaken, Viki. . . . Now about you and Mac——"

"What do you mean?"

"I don't mean further discussion at this point. I mean, are you coming to church with Reba and me tomorrow?"

"Today," Viki corrected. "Of course, if you want us." She paused, her eyes sparkled with mischief. "I've just told Mom I've a job in Boston. It starts the end of next week. So her way to bring me salvation is to threaten to cut off my allowance—of course with Dad's blessing. . . . Is church your solution?"

"No. I doubt if our minister could convert you to a more orthodox way of life. In his efforts to chasten he often drones on about youth. The last time his text was the evil and adulterous generation."

"How do you stand it?"

"We have an excellent organist and choir. I don't have to listen to anything else. And I was brought up in that old building."

Viki asked, "You're condoning my behavior? I'm sure Mom thinks so."

"I'm not condoning it, Viki, and I'm not condemning it." The blanket slipped to the floor, as she rose, walked over to her granddaughter, and touched her shoulder lightly. "I don't want you to be hurt. . . . Do you and Mac love each other?"

"We're in love, Gran."

"I realize that, but it's not quite the same, as you'll find out—probably the hard way. But what you're doing is very risky, and I don't mean the usual risk. Nowadays that's not as great, I suppose, as it used to be." She walked on past, opened the connecting door, and closed it behind her firmly.

 8

LUCY PEMBERTON WENT BACK to bed but not to sleep. She could do a good deal of thinking between now and breakfast—or not as much thinking as remembering. Most of her life she had avoided what she privately termed "unpleasant thinking" (which is not to say, negative). Impersonal thinking, on impersonal issues, was easy; she came of a long line of debaters, statesmen, and lawyers; people who loved discussions. Some of them, including her father, had enjoyed arguments. She did not. She was willing to face facts: facts like depression, business crises, illness—her infrequent own, her children's—even, at the end, Sam's. But never scenes; she would take a plane to Kenya to avoid one. Sam had known this and perhaps other people did. Did Viki, for one, Reba for another? Sam had said once, "How you duck and sidestep! You're a darling, evasive, elusive, exasperating woman, and I love you."

Once he had also said, "I wish you'd get good and mad more often."

"I don't have a temper, or if I fly into one, it's upsetting and unusual. I've a high boiling point."

"Oh, but you take it out in sneaky ways—icy shrugs,

88

eyebrow raising, or an edge to your voice. You get rid of the irritations, the annoyances. You're anything but repressed!"

She remembered now how he'd laughed when he said it.

Cynthia had just made a scene. It was curious to think of her, the self-possessed child, the self-possessed woman, boiling over. Lucy suspected now that she did so often. On the infrequent occasions when she'd done so as a child, it was her father who had gentled her down and Lucy who had left the room.

Ducking, sidestepping; nowadays they'd call it "copping out," she reflected.

What had she been supposed to do in this situation? Flail Viki with harsh words? Express shock, horror, disgust, bitter disappointment?

She was, in effect, an outsider. She had no right. . . .

Lucy's parents had been hardy, hearty, loving; a quarrelsome, fighting team. She'd had a good childhood, shared with two brothers and a sister, and had become accustomed to raised voices, table thumping, door slamming, and was none the worse for it. She simply didn't like noise and arguments, so she would creep quietly away until the storm passed. It had never been of long duration; the lightning ceased to flash, the thunder stilled, the sun came out, and her mother would be calling something familiar: "Supper's ready," "Go wash up," or "Aren't you ready for school?" or "How about a picnic?"

Perhaps that's why I'm not afraid of storms in nature, she thought, or hurricanes, floods, bolts of lightning, and I doubt I'd be frightened in an earthquake. I grew up believing all such manifestations pass, and you endure them. When the upheaval is caused by humans, you survive if you can just get away by yourself and don't interfere.

Her father had not brooked interference; if, during a family brouhaha, one of the children ventured into the ring, he had sent him or her flying out of it unless personally involved.

Lucy had been a vital, secretive child. She had passions: trees, flowers, books, animals, and movies. She rarely cried, except alone, reading something which moved her, or in the darkness of a motion-picture house.

"Who—except me—would have suspected you of thermal activity—most of which is underground?" Sam had once said.

She'd known him since childhood. He was eight years her senior, but he had a sister Lucy's age and they had played together. Lucy sometimes said, "Sam's very good-looking," and Rhoda would reply, "I suppose so." Or if Sam had condescended to tease them, his sister would exclaim, "That big lout!"

Lucy was ten when Sam graduated from high school and she went with Rhoda to the graduation. He was around that summer, working in the mills. During his four college years he was home for most vacations, and Lucy would see him on the streets, with a girl at a movie, or at the Pemberton house during a party, which she and Rhoda would watch from the upstairs landing.

Lucy remembered herself at seventeen . . . with long legs and long pale brown hair . . . having a sundae with Rhoda, when Sam came in with a couple of friends. He'd stopped by their little corner table, remarked, "You've grown some, Lucy," and had then gone to the counter, saying, "I'll pay Rhoda's and Lucy's checks." He left a tip, bought a pipe, and departed.

"What's got into him?" inquired Rhoda. "He's never picked up our checks before."

Sam was twenty-five then and he'd been working in the mills for three straight years. He was, so his father informed Lucy's father, doing very well indeed, but like most of his friends, he enlisted in the army. The year was 1917.

That autumn, when Lucy was still seventeen, she went off to college. Her mother had insisted. Rhoda remained at home, but the girls communicated by letter and saw each other during Lucy's holidays.

Now and then, when Rhoda was writing to her brother and Lucy happened to be with her, Rhoda would say, "I told Sam you'd add a P.S." So she'd write something like: "Dear Sam, your family worries because they haven't heard from you lately. I hope you're all right. Love, Lucy."

Peaceable was soon almost devoid of young males; there were the 4-Fs and the older men; there were a few who had deferments because of their employment in the Pemberton Mills which had substantial army orders. And every girl in town who could write was writing to a dozen soldiers, sailors, fliers—some of them strangers.

In 1919 Sam was discharged, and returned to Peaceable and the mills. He had been wounded and would have for the rest of his life a slight limp which in no way handicapped him. He'd been, according to Rhoda, engaged twice. Once to a girl he'd met at camp. She married someone else, and the Pembertons hadn't even known her. And once, by letter, to Olive Powell, whom Lucy knew by sight. Sam and Olive had been, as Rhoda put it, "off and on for years." But Olive had eloped with a band leader. Rhoda found this reprehensible desertion of her brother highly romantic.

Lucy graduated at twenty-one, and was planning to teach. She had been accepted for a post in a small private elementary school near Boston. Meantime, she had the summer. . . .

She had no idea when she fell in love with Sam. It seemed to her later that she'd always been involved with the Pemberton's only son, but perhaps she merely dreamed it.

How had it actually started, and when?

By mid-July she was engaged to be married. The fact that Sam's mother disapproved didn't worry her—or Sam. His father thought Lucy a little young, but he liked her; her parents were pleased. Rhoda was in heaven. She'd always wanted a sister.

Lucy resigned her post, to the dismay of the headmistress, and was wholly happy. The Pembertons had given them a small old house on two pleasant acres, and Lucy's parents had furnished it. The wedding was to be in October. Sam would get a holiday from the mills, and they were going south, to a plantation turned guest house, on their wedding trip.

In August, Lucy went to Rhode Island to visit her father's sister, Aunt Gwen, for a month. Her mother thought her too thin, and the family physician, young Doctor Harmon, said, "Girls about to be married run themselves ragged—parties, clothes, excitement. Get her away from Peaceable and see she's built up."

Aunt Gwen was an amiable, scatterbrained, delightful woman, with a large silent husband who adored her. They were childless and the summer place on Rhode Island was on the water . . . sun and bathing, sleeping late, being coaxed to eat, and writing to Sam every day; that was the program. Lucy gained five pounds, and her fair skin was apricot-tanned and her pale brown hair sun-streaked. And Sam came every weekend.

So that's how it happened, if anything really just happens.

Aunt Gwen and Uncle Roger went out a good deal. They were dedicated bridge players, club members, and golfers. There was evening bridge often at their home or the homes of friends, and Aunt Gwen would say, "The children won't mind being left alone, Roger."

Even when it was their turn to entertain—for quite high stakes—their card-playing friends, Lucy and Sam, if he were there, could slip away, go down and sit on the dock, walk the beach, or shut themselves up in the little guesthouse, used, together with the garage apartment, for visiting chauffeurs. They always returned to the main house before the guests left. When Sam wasn't there, Lucy, as assistant to Aunt Gwen's invaluable butler, would provide unnecessary but attractive help in bringing drinks and emptying ashtrays.

With all that space—and all that freedom—making love became as natural as breathing. That was the euphemism . . . as if any one can "make" love as one makes a drink or a cake.

For Lucy, it was a revelation of that paradox; pleasure in pain, pain in pleasure.

After almost fifty years she remembered this and some of the brief occasional words spoken, after long silences: "Of course, this is terribly wrong." That was Lucy.

"Do you believe that?" Sam had asked and presently Lucy answered, "No, I don't."

Aunt Gwen had long since been gathered to her ancestors. Lucy had wondered—particularly at the funeral, which she and Sam had attended—if now Aunt Gwen's new knowledge extended to the past.

Tonight she thought of Viki and her scruples: "Not here, Gran."

Lucy had not experienced completion immediately, nor had she felt frustration. When in reply to her whispered, "I'm so happy," Sam had said quietly, "You'll be happier, darling," she'd been astonished. "There's more?"

On Sam's last weekend at Aunt Gwen's—he was driving Lucy home Sunday evening—the two put on their bathing suits (Lucy's, a Kellerman, was considered rather daring), Aunt Gwen had a lunch basket packed for them, and they went for a last beach walk and swim. "Keep your robes on," Aunt counseled, "or you'll burn to a crisp."

This time they walked through salt marshes, shallow water, and clam mud and around the bend, where a sudden sandspit—narrow and white and always deserted because in those days private property was just that—projected suddenly into the water. At high tide it was covered. Lucy had been there often with her aunt and uncle, and with them and Sam, once. Now they had it to themselves.

Wading birds, and shells; beach grass growing. No shade; nothing but sun, sand and water; no noise but the whisper of waves, the crying of gulls. Very far out, they could see boats. Boats did not come near there except an occasional fisherman, rowing, and even these stayed away from the sandspit; shallow water and a great many rocks were deterrents.

Seaweeds drifted; transparent jellyfish and little minnows swam, and white clouds fashioned changing shapes in the blue sky.

"Look, Sam, that's a house!"

But he was looking at her, taking her in his arms, saying, "Tomorrow we have to go back. You'll be busy; your mother will drive you crazy; your house will be full of moronic girls; my mother will be going around with a face as long as your arm, and eventually there'll be the wedding, before which I'll manage to get drunk with the boys. I'm going to be lonely, Lucy, and until October, we'll never be alone as we are now."

Then he said, "That silly bathing suit!"

AFTERWARDS, THE SUITS DRYING ON THE SAND, they wrapped themselves in their toweling robes and Sam asked, "Why did you cry?"

94

"Because I was happy."

He said, "Dare you to swim, as is."

So they swam and then dried with the towels they'd brought. Lucy's heavy hair was wet and her face shining with water and sun and fulfilled love. There was salt on her lips.

Young and healthy, they had lunch, sedate in their voluminous garments, and presently she went to sleep, her head against his bare shoulder. She remembered often, as now, waking and seeing his expression as he looked down at her. She would not forget it; not ever. She was to see it many times in their years together.

She could not then, or now, describe it, even to herself—very grave, almost anxious, and informed with such tenderness that her heart turned over. But then he smiled. He said, "You're awake? We'd better get going; the tide's started in."

September came, flamed, and went in Peaceable. Doctor Harmon was satisfied with Lucy's five pounds and her glowing health. He said to her mother, "Now if she doesn't collapse before next month, we'll get her through."

He was Sam's age; a native of Peaceable; married with one child; a good hardworking man, who cared about people.

Before the wedding Lucy's mother had what was known as a "little talk" with her daughter. She was sensible, blunt, and embarrassed; and Lucy listened, her face serious, her heart laughing. She saw Sam only when he came to supper, or when she went to the Pembertons', anxious to ingratiate herself with his formidable mother. Sometimes they managed to go for a drive, unchaperoned, but they were very circumspect. This was Peaceable.

Then the wedding on a beautiful day. It was warm in the sun, cool at night, and the oak leaves were still holding their dusty pink, pale brown color. The church was crowded. The reception was at Lucy's house. Rhoda, maid of honor, cried steadily through the ceremony and had a touch too much champagne at the reception.

Prohibition had not extended to the private wine cellars all over America which still retained a smattering of wines and brandies, whiskeys, and liqueurs. Few prosperous people in Peaceable bought from bootleggers. Some who did, regretted it. There were no speakeasies in Peaceable, but Sam and his friends knew of some outside of the town.

There was dancing at the reception, to a small orchestra, and Rhoda stopped crying.

"Let's get out of here," said Sam, in his bride's ear.

They changed upstairs, Sam in her parent's room and Lucy in her own. The car had been brought around minus tin cans, signs, or streamers. Sam had seen to that. And, in a flurry of embraces, good wishes, and rice, they left while the orchestra was playing last year's hit, "Avalon."

"Thank God," said Sam devoutly. Lucy had gone on thanking Him ever since.

They spent the night in Boston at the Copley Plaza, and on the following day took the train for the South, having garaged the car for the duration.

That night, in Boston, she'd said, "We must have been crazy."

"Of course," Sam agreed comfortably.

"I've been thinking, ever since Aunt Gwen's . . . anything might have happened." She paused. Her mother had taken her to Dr. Harmon and he had explained to her certain matters about which she had known only vaguely. She was now equipped with a device which she had no intention of using—it scared her—and with other information.

"So?" asked Sam, lying beside her.

She told him about Doctor Harmon.

96

"That Pete!" he said. "Were you embarrassed?"

"Yes. And then it dawned on me that at Aunt Gwen's, you didn't——"

He interrupted serenely, "Nope. I was hoping you'd get pregnant."

"Sam Pemberton!"

"Yes, Mrs. Pemberton?"

"Why?" she'd asked faintly.

"I hate big weddings. It was a long time to October. We could have run off somewhere and been married. Damn sight easier and less expensive for my present in-laws."

"Well, I didn't," she'd reminded him indignantly.

"Not my fault, darling."

She said, "I never gave it a thought, really." And hearing him laugh, added, "It gives me the creeps now to think of the risk. . . . I suppose I thought, if I thought about it at all, that you had some sort of magic—well—formula."

"Magic, all right. Come here, and shut up."

The Peaceable years, in the small house. She learned to cook more than passably; her mother had taught her the basics, but Sam had taught her more. He was a naturally gifted cook when it suited him to throw her out of the kitchen, remarking, "You can do the cleaning up." The good years, alone, until Jack was born in 1924, and Cynthia in '28. (There'd been a miscarriage in between).

Now she thought: I was a complete failure as a mother.

There are mother-women, she thought further, and wife-women. Maybe some can be fifty-fifty. I couldn't.

In the autumn of twenty-nine—with Cynthia blooming into beauty ("Thought she'd never have any hair," Sam had said relieved) and Jack a lively, noisy five-year-old, chasing his dog or Lucy's cat, getting into ditches, poison ivy; sweet, demanding, laughing more than he cried—the crash came.

Tightened belts; men laid off; Sam working long, hard hours; Lucy learning to stick to a budget. No outside assistance in the house. Sam helped with the heavy cleaning, and took what time he could to cut some of the grass. "Let the rest go into meadow," he'd said. Jack tagged along after him, and Jack's paternal grandfather for whom the boy had been named would turn up to ask, "Anything I can do?"

Hard years, anxious; but she thought: Not really. We had each other.

Cynthia and Edward didn't have each other. And Viki . . . ?

If she's lucky, Lucy thought, she'll eventually have someone, probably not Mac, for which I'd be sorry.

During the Depression, there was radio. At times during more recent years Lucy had found herself wishing that it had never been relegated to second place. Radio was a voice in the night while waiting for Sam to come home; it was excitement and drama, and you had to use your imagination; it wasn't all spelled out for you.

Then the tide turned, with the inauguration of F.D.R., the banks closing, and the start of a new era.

The mills prospered again; Sam's parents died; Lucy and Sam moved into the Pemberton house, and Reba came to run it for them. The children grew up. Jack enlisted in the Marines at eighteen, and was killed. Cynthia went to her mother's college and was married in 1950. And Sam and Lucy traveled when he could get away: to Florida for fishing, Maine for more fishing, to New York for plays, shops, restaurants; and to California on Mill business. The first time they'd gone it had been by transcontinental train. Lucy had liked that: the stateroom moving through dark nights, the sound of the wheels, the deep cough which had replaced the warning whistle, the stops in the night—"Where are we, Sam?" . . . "God knows, Go back to sleep"—but she'd pull up the shade and look out at moving figures on a platform and listen to voices. And by day seeing the sliding, changing landscape; eating in the elegant diner. . . . She often thought of the Twentieth Century Limited and the demitasse of black coffee served the instant the steward took you to a table and before you'd ordered breakfast; and of the overnight stops in Chicago, where they always stayed at the Blackstone so they could walk on Michigan and look into shop windows, and see old friends for dinner.

Planes were fine, but you couldn't sleep with your husband on a plane, even in the days when there were berths.

And then nineteen fifty-nine.

"Lets go to Spain—I'm taking a month off—we can see Rhoda."

Rhoda had married a young man in the State Department a year or so after Lucy's wedding, and had lived mainly abroad because her husband had been attached to various embassies. She had come home now and then with her children; but they were now grown and scattered. Her husband had been killed in an automobile accident, and except for brief visits to Peaceable, Rhoda chose to remain in Jávea, her husband's last port.

Lucy and Sam flew Iberia to Madrid for a few days, and from there to Valencia, where the travel agent had arranged for a car they would drive to the Costa Blanca.

"Unless," Rhoda had said over the transatlantic telephone, "you want to stay in Valencia for the fiesta; if so, I'll have to get you reservations way ahead."

Sam decided that he'd rather drive straight south. Cynthia and Edward had come to the airport to see them off, always a rather fidgety process unlike ship sailings, and on the plane Sam had said, "Cynthia isn't happy."

"What makes you think that?"

"I don't think it; I feel it. Has she said anything to you?"

"No, but then she rarely does. . . . We've always liked Edward and now they have the little girls."

"Something's wrong. I dunno what. If it is, do you think kids can compensate, for a woman?"

"Not for me," she said after a moment, "but I don't know about Cynthia."

In Valencia, the car and the pleasant representative of a rental company, who assured them he knew Mrs. Emerson well—a most delightful lady. He gave them careful directions, with Sam muttering, "Let's get on with it," to no one in particular.

It was March; it was spring. Rice paddies on the outskirts of Valencia. A two-hour drive past orange and lemon groves, the air heavily fragrant, and the two-lane highway lined with yellow iris.

Nearing Jávea—the mountains in the distance, with snow upon their peaks and the Mediterranean on the right—Sam had said, "My God, it's beautiful!" and then, "I think when we get back home you should have a talk with Cynthia."

"You're fretting. I'm sure she's all right . . . and I've never been able to talk with her—I mean seriously, problems, all that. I've tried a time or two. She resents it. She shuts against me like a fist."

She'd remembered then their conversation prior to Cynthia's wedding and added, "I offered conventional confidences before she was married."

"Facts of life?" he asked, amused. "In this day and age?"

"No, not biology lessons. I just tried to tell her how wonderful her relationship with Edward could be, how she would grow into it, as natural a flowering as anything in nature. Sam, she was embarrassed; she cut me short; she didn't want to hear me out."

Sam had said, "It's hard for kids to realize that their parents

100

have a relationship—not necessarily a good one, darling—but, anyway, one which is apart from their children, one which is private and their own. They seem to see parents as merely parents."

"Well, when we get back, perhaps she'll be ready to tell me if anything's wrong . . . not that I believe it. I'll try, anyway," she'd promised.

She hadn't tried.

It was at that point that Sam had said, "The next turn is Gata—left."

The last five miles led them through the citrus and olive groves along a narrower curved road to Jávea.

It was a fishing village; one section was the old town; the other, the Port. White houses with red-tiled roofs, facing south, overlooking the bay and beaches. All the houses had terraced grounds, an abundance of trees, and huge urns of flowers. Rhoda's, on the hill, was very like a number of others and it had a heated swimming pool. Her view was superb. And so was Rhoda, crying, glad to see them, looking much as they'd last seen her with her short white hair, a round pretty figure, and sun-brown face.

That evening after they'd unpacked, had drinks and a late dinner—it had cooled off and the fireplace logs were blazing—Rhoda had asked, "How's business, Sam?"

"You get the stockholders' reports."

"I know. But you might add a little to the dull, if encouraging, pages."

He said, "You know I retired as President three years ago, but stayed on as Chairman of the Board. Fellowes is an exceptionally sound man, considerably younger than I, progressive, and yet cautious. He'll do fine; so will the rest of the team. I'm going to retire as Chairman after I get back. I wanted to a while ago, but they wouldn't let me."

"What in the world will you do?"

"Travel, play golf, sleep late mornings, and make love to my wife!"

They spent a wonderful holiday with Rhoda. Sam was enchanted with the long siestas, the port hotel with the terrace where they had drinks, the pier and the fishermen. It was too cold, as yet, to swim in the Mediterranean—the pool sufficed; and he told Rhoda, "We'll be back."

He liked Rhoda's friends, and they liked him and Lucy and just before they left Sam said to his sister, "Suppose you snoop around and see if there's anything for sale—a good little house, for Lucy and me. Not a lot of spare rooms either. Or if there's no house—property. Perhaps we could build. Lucy and I have been talking it over." He grinned and spread his arms. "This is our kind of place, for winters and maybe longer, and we'd make you oversee it when we took off for London—Lucy has a thing about London—or went home, or whatever. . . . How about it?"

Rhoda had said, "It would be wonderful. See that he sticks to it, Lucy."

He had stuck to it, but not for long. In 1960, the first coronary, the slow recovery, and then the second.

Lucy remembered, listening to the birds singing in the dawn, how he'd said, "We won't have our castle in Spain, darling."

He was wrong. They had it, for many years.

Tears, unusual for her, slipped down her cheeks. She turned over and put her face in the pillow. She thought: If you'd stayed with me, Sam, you could have made things right for Cynthia, or helped her make them right for herself.

She slept lightly, uneasily, knowing that she must soon go down and face breakfast with Viki, Mac, and Reba, and without Cynthia.

9

WHEN LUCY REACHED HER DINING ROOM, no one was there. She looked at the dark shining wood of the oval table, the silver, the crystal, the marmalade jar with the ceramic bees, the pretty floral mats and neatly folded matching napkins, "You've got to come to it, Lucy," Reba had said. "Saves washing; and Nettie is pretty unreliable." So paper mats and napkins because Nettie who came to do the laundry twice a week, relied periodically on gin.

Reba came in from the kitchen. "Where's everyone?" asked Lucy and Reba said, "You look terrible."

"I suppose so. I didn't sleep well. Oh . . . Cynthia will have a tray in her room."

"Cyn's gone," Reba reported. "Maybe an hour or more ago. I heard the garage doors slam, looked out, and she was streaking out the driveway."

Lucy said, after a moment, "She told me last night"— nearer morning, she thought—"that she was going home today, but she didn't say when."

Viki shot downstairs, and Reba thought: I guess nobody slept much. Viki and Lucy look as if they'd been over Niagara Falls. She always used that expression; it was one of

Sam's. He claimed he'd known a man who had done it, and Reba had inquired, "Well how did he look?" and Sam had answered gravely, "Wet."

"Mom not coming to breakfast?" asked Viki and added, "Don't answer that. Of course she isn't."

"Your mother has left," Lucy told her, and sat down, slumping a little. "Reba heard her go; I didn't."

Reba said, "You two need your coffee," took it from the hot plate, poured it for Lucy, for Viki, and herself. "Where's your young man, Viki?"

"I hollered at him," Viki said. "Maybe he's gone back to sleep."

He hadn't. He clattered downstairs, and said, "Good morning, everyone." His smiling glance at Viki was a translation of a light kiss. " 'Fraid I'm late."

Reba asked, "Eggs anyone?" and Viki rallied to order, "One, soft-boiled." And Mac asked, "Could mine be fried? . . . two, if you insist."

Reba vanished to inform Sadie, Lucy started making toast, and Mac asked, "Isn't Mrs. Warren coming down?"

"She left for home early," Lucy told him, and Viki said, "I—well she was waiting up for me last night, Mac, and I blew it."

His expression was strange—relief, apprehension, shock.

And Lucy said, "You and Viki can talk about it later. I suggest a walk in the garden. Are you still going to church with us, Viki?"

"Of course, with or without Mac."

"I'd like to go," Mac said and Lucy nodded. "We'll have midday dinner," she told him. "I never used to; Viki's grandfather disliked it. But now it's easier." She shrugged. "Sadie's off Sunday afternoons, so we scratch up some supper for ourselves. . . . Are you staying over, Viki?"

"If it's all right with you, I thought I'd start back after lunch tomorrow."

Lucy looked at Mac, and said, "I wish you could too, but I suppose you'll want to leave this afternoon."

"Yes, Mrs. Pemberton, I'd planned to. I have to be at work tomorrow," Mac answered.

Reba came back, Sadie followed. Mac regarded his eggs. He'd thought he was hungry, but he wasn't. What had Viki said? What had her mother said? What was Mrs. Pemberton thinking?

She was thinking: I suppose we'll get through today and tomorrow, and Viki asked, "You sure you don't mind my staying?"

"I'd love it," Lucy said, smiling at her. "I've nothing to do—no engagements that is—until Friday."

After breakfast Mac and Viki walked in the garden. "What's this all about?" he asked.

"Let's go into the summerhouse and sit down," Viki suggested. "You'll be furious with me."

"It won't be the first time," he said and tried to laugh but did not succeed.

The summerhouse was cool, but sun slanted in, and the wisteria, done with this season's blooming, was thick on the rustic walls and damp with dew.

"Shoot," said Mac. He did not put his arms around her. This did not seem the right time.

She told him briefly. Then she said, finally, "I had to tell her, Mac."

"In a way, I'm glad. And your grandmother?"

"She knows too."

"That figures."

"Mom woke her up and dragged her in to give her a resumé."

"And . . .?"

"And nothing, really. After Mom boiled out and went to her room, I talked with Gran. She warned me that what we've done—are doing—is risky. We already know that. She didn't lecture me or throw me out in the snow if that's what you're thinking. She—well—she's not an interfering person. I suspect," said Viki, "it's easier for her."

"What do you mean by that?"

"You'd have to know her to understand. She just doesn't want any part of a bad scene."

"What about your father?"

Viki said slowly, "I suppose when he comes home, Mom will tell him. I'll probably be in Boston by then."

"You mean you're still going to be in Boston?"

"Certainly. They can disinherit me," said Viki and laughed, "but I can still have my Boston summer. I won't be living at the Ritz, of course, but then I never intended to. I'll get along. I have my piggy bank."

She was to share an apartment, Mac knew, with another girl, one of her classmates, who had a job at the University that summer. She'd said when she wrote him, "I don't know her well, but she's all right. Straight and all that. Her people go to Marblehead summers. She'll be with them weekends."

He straightened up, moving his shoulders as if freed of a burden, and Viki said, "Remember, whatever happens, we'll still have our summer." She leaned forward and kissed his cheek. "Don't worry. . . . Now I'd better go back and see if there's anything I can wear to church, something respectable. I'd hate to disgrace Reba."

"You're a very strange kid," said Mac. "I'd have thought you'd be beside yourself."

"I don't like me well enough."

"But most girls——"

"I'm not most girls," Viki informed him. "And this

106

isn't the nineteenth century. I'm sorry for Mom. She thinks it is, you know. . . . Come on back to the house." She rose, holding out her hand. "I'd race you but, as of now, I don't have the strength. Last night—the Mom scene—was a doozy. Mac, if we don't get a chance to talk alone again, here, I'll let you know what shuttle I'm taking to Boston on Friday. I'll have the weekend to get settled before I go to work."

"I'll try to meet you."

"No. It might be a wrong time for you."

"What's your hurry now?" he asked. "It's still nowhere near church time."

"Near enough, and I've a chore or two to do."

He thought: She's uneasy with me. Whatever her mother said to her last night got to her.

On the way through the biggest garden, Viki said, "It was fun, being here with you for a while . . . seeing you at dinner, taking that fatal drive and, before, all that listening to music with Gran. She's a doll. She tries so hard to go along with what's happening, even if she doesn't always, really, dig it."

"Well, she knows it's Nowville and she has to live in it," Mac said. "I'm grateful to her for having me here." He stopped in the sunny garden. "This is a beautiful place," he added.

"I love it," Viki told him, "and not just because I've been coming here since before I can remember. There's something about the surroundings and in the house itself. The house is quiet, no matter how much noise anyone makes in it. There's a feeling of—well—occupancy . . . of many people having lived and died here, loving, hating, quarreling, making up, laughing, crying."

"Did your grandfather build it?"

"No, his father. There was a lot of land and a small house already here. He rebuilt it and enlarged it. I've been in much older houses, and in elegant contemporaries and in more spectacular settings. Gran's place isn't manicured and never has been—not anyway since she and Gramp lived here. Fields, meadows, trees dying and falling—they aren't always cut up for firewood—and underbrush. So it isn't spit and polish inside or out. Gran's kept it up, but there's not much help to be had and, even here, it costs an arm and a leg. I like it this way, comfortable and right."

They went along into the house and he thought—without envy, but with a small ache of sorrow—how different her life had been from his. He had no complaint about his own. He was happy with his family and his work. His world was as wide as hers and as full of promise. He too had seen more impressive houses, than this one—traveling, working, on vacations, in Boston, and nearby. He'd never been inside of one except with his parents or friends, as paying tourists. Had he grown up in circumstances similar to Viki's would he have understood her better? He thought not.

When the time came, they went to church. Reba in a hat from another era, a flowered dress and jacket; Lucy in a white linen suit, and with a band of black velvet around her shapely head. They both wore gloves. Viki was herself, in her full skirt and Mexican blouse. The organist was fine; the choir, almost as good; the earnest clergyman, inoffensive. Reba was probably the only one of the four who listened to him; the others thought their own thoughts. Lucy said a private prayer in her mind; it had to do with Viki, with Cynthia and Edward, and it was quite informal. She said silently, "They do need help, Lord," and afterwards, walking out into the sunlight, wondered, if she had not, in reality, directed the petition to Sam.

Handshaking, introductions (Mac to minister) and greetings mainly for Viki, as a number of people in the congregation had known her for years. Dan Burton and his wife were there. He hailed Mac, spoke to Lucy and Reba, and said, "I wish young Dan could have come."

"Where is he?" Viki asked. "I'm home. Why isn't he?"

"Went off with some buddies on a camping trip," Dan said. "Promised he'd be home by the first to help me at the station. The summer people are already arriving and I'll have my hands full."

"And with any luck, your tanks empty," said Lucy, smiling.

They left, and in the car, she said. "Thanks, children. You must have been very bored."

"Why?" asked Reba. "It was a nice service. Mr. Tremont's a good preacher.

Lucy thought: Well, sweetness and light, especially the sweetness . . . very diabetic-making. Aloud, "Yes, of course," she agreed.

"She misses her old flame," said Reba suddenly.

Lucy laughed. "Reba means Mr. Grant. Reba has flattering fancies about me. Thinks practically everyone, from our garbage man on, is one of my old flames."

"Well, aren't they?" asked Mac, smiling. "And now you have a new one."

"That's very handsome of you," Lucy told him. She added that Ellsworth Grant had been a longtime friend, and for many years pastor of the church.

"And of course," said Reba, "there's Peter Harmon."

"He's Gran's doctor," Viki explained to Mac. . . . "Seen him lately, Gran?"

"We had dinner with the Grants a few weeks ago, which reminds me, Reba. We must ask Pete and Winnie to come to us."

Home, and out of the churchgoing garments, Viki

appearing in shorts, Lucy modeling one of her pants suits, in pale blue, and Reba saying, "She'll be wearing shorts next."

"Hot pants?" Viki suggested.

Presently they went into the study for Lucy's sherry. Reba never had her one beer on Sunday. Mac and Viki had tomato juice. "I," said Lucy, "seem to be the only one indulging." She looked at her sherry on the rocks, adding, "Reminds me of Spain."

After dinner, Reba excused herself, to help Sadie so that she could get away. And Lucy said, "I hate good-byes so I'm going up and lie down, Mac. I'm glad you came to see us and I hope I'll see you again. Take him walking, Viki, and then see him off properly."

Mac said, "I have to get my belongings. May I walk you upstairs, Mrs. Pemberton?"

"A pleasure," said Lucy, as they went sedately up the broad stairs together.

At her door she stopped. She said, "I'm not going to give you or Viki any advice, Mac. Young people rarely took it in my day and I doubt Viki's mother's generation did either. I've already told Viki that I think extracurricular relationships are dangerous; the road's full of pitfalls, ambushes, also dead ends. However, it may be different now, from what I read and hear." She held out her hand, noting as he took it that his was a good hand, strong, masculine—and added, "I wish you both good fortune, wherever the road leads."

"Thank you," he said, not smiling, "and for everything else."

She went into her room; the door closed. He went to his and looked around him. I wonder if I'll ever see it again, he thought, and shook his head. I guess the answer is negative. He tossed his things into the flight bag and went downstairs again. Reba came into the hall. She asked unnecessarily, "You going? . . . Well, have a good trip, but drive carefully—it's

Sunday." She took off her apron, wiped her hands on it, shook hands, and went back to where she had come from.

Mac was alone in the hall. It smelled of roses and wax and fresh air. He looked around and then went into the study and the living room, calling "Viki?"

"I'm out here," she called and he found her sitting on the steps. She said, "Walk me down to the stone wall—that one, the nearest——"

Mac's car was where he'd left it, near the house. He tossed the flight bag in, went back to the steps and pulled Viki to her feet. They walked to the stone wall. "Sit awhile. It's pleasant here," she said.

Sun from the sky, shade from the big trees. "Take it easy on the way back. It's Sunday," Viki said.

"So Reba reminded me. I hate to go. I went upstairs with your grandmother. She wished us both good luck."

"We're our own luck."

"Somehow, it embarrasses me—being with her, I mean, after last night. I don't think I'd have felt the same about your mother if I'd seen her again. I was mad as hell at her for putting you through that scene," Mac said.

"Forget it," Viki advised. "I could take it, and suppose I'll have to take more of the same."

"Plus your father."

She knitted her brows, unraveled them and regarded him with serene eyes. "That will be different," she said. "I don't know what to expect, or whether I'll see him before Friday. If not, it's only a postponement. I daresay Mom will try to send him flying to Boston . . . but he makes up his own mind. If he chases after me, it won't be her doing but his. Do stop fretting. It's no big thing, although Mom thinks so, and probably Dad will. Kiss me hello, leave me sitting here, a wall-flower." She laughed, "I forgot to look for poison ivy. . . . Go on back to your crate."

111

"It's a good little car," he said, with affection.

"So, okay. . . . Wave as you go by. Be seein' you."

She watched him walk across the grass to the car, watched him drive around the curve, saw him wave, waved in reply, and sat there reflecting on her future, his future. But why look past this summer? she thought. All anyone can count on is right now. In that case the weeks ahead were future, hence presumably uncertain.

She wondered briefly where her father was; she thought she knew with whom. How long would that last? How long did anything last? Her parents' marriage had been fraying at the seams for a long time. Her grandparents' had lasted . . . as far as I know, Viki thought. It must have. But no outsider ever saw the secret fabric of a relationship, just the outward appearance of the garment.

She wondered what her mother was doing. She must be home by now or nearly so, unless she stopped along the way. Why would she, except for gas or a sandwich? Viki shivered. Perhaps she'd had an accident or deliberately driven over a cliff or into a stone wall, such as the one Viki was sitting on. "You," said Viki to herself, "are just being dramatic. It isn't in her nature to do anything like that."

What did she know about her mother's nature? Or her father's or, for that matter, her own or anyone's "Talk about mysteries," she reminded herself. "If anything's more mysterious than people, I'll eat it."

Tomorrow she'd have to start home. She dreaded it. She wished she could be transported to Boston magically, with her unpacked-at-home luggage in her hands . . . wished she could go straight from Peaceable to Boston, skipping Westchester, her mother, her father—if he came home—and even Jenny. Jenny horsing around with or without a steed, released from school, doing her own thing, but around, inquisitive, often maddening! She wondered also how she herself would

112

get along with a comparatively strange girl in a strange apartment. Karen Banks had said, when they made the arrangement, first tentatively at Blue Mountain, then by letter. "Don't expect anything fancy, but there's a good stove—hope you can cook—and the other conveniences. We probably won't see much of each other, but I'm not hard to get along with, and I don't think you are either."

She wondered how often she'd see Mac and under what circumstances?

Now she removed herself from the wall and rubbed her small round behind. No bed of roses, the New Hampshire rocks. Walking toward the house she began to think of herself descriptively in the third person: ". . . the lovely young girl with her copper-colored hair unbound in the breeze, walked lightly toward her grandmother's residence, the big bad wolf having departed with a grinding of gears and noxious fumes. The girl was intelligent, misguided, happily ruined, reckless but lovable, and quite without fear."

When she reached the house, she was laughing aloud.

Lucy had heard the car drive away; she heard—all her windows stood open—Viki laughing. She thought; she certainly isn't heartbroken, and she isn't afraid, and I haven't detected a trace of guilt.

If my parent's or Sam's or even Aunt Gwen had caught Sam and me, I would have been scared out of what wits I had. Not Sam—he would have been delighted—no big wedding, just a quiet gathering of the shocked clan.

With Mac, she thought, I was courteous, hospitable, and quite charming—besides I like him. She smiled, remembering Reba's remark about "old flames" and Mac's saying he was a new one. Sam always said I was the vainest woman he ever knew, she reflected.

Would Mac and Viki have respected her if she'd thrown them both out of the house?

113

Respect? What was it? Lucy liked to be respected for what she was or, at least, for the image she created. She would bet her shares in the mill that Viki hadn't said to Mac, "But now you won't respect me!" And God knows Lucy hadn't said that to Sam, even way back when.

Maybe I should have said more to Mac, standing with him at my door. But what? . . . "Mac, I made the same mistake as Viki."

And if he'd asked, "Were you punished for it?" she would have had to say, "No." And if he'd inquired, "Have you punished yourself, have you been unhappy about it all these years?" her answer in all honesty would have been the same.

There was never a happier woman, she thought, until ten years ago; and even the ten have been happy, remembering.

So I didn't say anything to him except a polite, cliché warning. How could I?

She thought again of Reba's old flames remark, took one of Peter Harmon's pills, and lay still, waiting for the nagging little pain that had troubled her lately to be obliterated. So I copped out again, she thought.

⟶ 10

REBA ALSO HEARD Mac's car drive off. She'd helped Sadie wash up, looked in the refrigerator and figured out what to have for supper. Sadie sometimes stayed overnight, Sundays, with relatives. And Thursdays she had the day off from breakfast until whatever time she cose to return at night. Now Reba asked, "Why don't you pack a bag and stay the night? No one here but me, Mrs. Pemberton and Viki. I'll see to breakfast."

Sadie was a good cook. They couldn't afford to lose her, and they might when the summer people came nosing around making inquiries and offering more money. Lucy paid enough for her help as it was; they had good hours. Sadie had her own room and bath, eventually they'd both have their Social Security checks. No matter what the papers said about the precarious plight of the still employed, as well as that of the unemployed, they had it a lot better than they used to.

She saw Sadie off, and then went into her own little apartment which Sam had fixed up for her: a single bedroom, small living room, and bath.

Reba couldn't remember when she hadn't known Sam. Her parents had a farm upstate. Reba had taught elementary school until her mother became ill with a long terminal illness. Then she gave up teaching, helped on the farm and cooked for her father and the hired men, sang in the little church, sold vegetables, flowers, and eggs. Sam would come for a week, or a few days, to fish with his father's youngest cousin, Reba's father. He was five years older than Reba. When he went to war, she wrote to him, and worried; when he came back, he came to see them. Reba went to his wedding, and stayed at the Pemberton house. When her father died, Sam came and made the funeral arrangements. Lucy was pregnant with Cynthia and couldn't come; she had to be careful because of the earlier miscarriage. And Sam had asked, "What'll you do now, Reba?"

"Sell the farm and get a job in Keaton."

Keaton was the nearest town.

"Teaching?"

"No, I've been out of it too long. But I'm a good housekeeper, and I think a good saleswomen," she'd told him.

"I'll ask around. Hold out for a good price. Things are booming; it's a good time to sell, but hang on to the money."

"Savings bank," she promised, "but if I come by a little extra, I'd like to invest it in the Mills."

"We'll talk about it when the time comes."

She'd sold, at more than a good price; so into the bank as promised, and some in the Mills.

And she'd taken a position as housekeeper in Keaton's good hotel, which stayed open all year: summers for vacationers and transients; salesmen, off season.

The hotel had closed during the winters after the crash but remained open, with some rooms closed and a smaller staff, summers. People had been coming there for years, and enough continued to do so. Reba was housekeeper still, but winters she took what work she could get, as cook in the diner, as aide in Keaton's hospital, helper and sometime cook in the nursing home. When out of work, she lived simply, in the small apartment she'd rented over Handy's garage, and in which she had some of her own furniture. Sam came now and then to see her. He sent her Christmas and birthday checks and then, when the recovery set in, and he and Lucy moved to the big house, Lucy wrote Reba and asked her if she would come live with them, manage the house, and help with the kids. She and Sam wanted her so much.

So she'd come and was still here.

When Lucy and Sam went off on trips, Reba ran the house and looked after the children, if they were home. They weren't always. Jack went to a war and did not return; Cynthia went off to college. Reba remembered when Cyn and Edward were married, right in this house. And Lucy and Sam had taken her to stay in New York; she'd seen Viki and Jenny shortly after each was born, and at frequent intervals ever since. She had been alone in the house, except for the current cook and housemaid, when Sam and Lucy went to Spain.

Now and then Sam had gone off by himself on business. "Look after Lucy, Reba," he'd say; "she isn't very strong."

She was as strong as a horse, except for the miscarriage, which Reba had always thought Lucy's fault—overdoing, driving her car, in those days, like a maniac, going dancing with Sam in her condition, But Sam had worried about her. I couldn't look fragile, Reba had often thought, if my life depended on it; maybe not even if I were dying. How Lucy manages it, God knows, I don't.

Sam had left Reba a legacy, beyond the money he willed her, and which she had willed to his grandchildren. He had left her Lucy. The last time Reba had seen him, in the hospital, he'd sent Lucy from the room and held fast to Reba's hand. He'd said, "Promise me something."

"Sam, don't talk."

"Just . . . stay with Lucy; look after her."

"I promise."

117

"Lean down." She had done so, and he kissed her cheek as he had done so many times for so many years. "I don't know what we would have done without you, Reba," he said.

She'd seen Lucy through the funeral, Cynthia coming, Edward, the girls, the many friends. She'd slept next door to her, listening to her cry herself to sleep. She had tried to make her eat, special things in small amounts. When summer came, she made her go into the garden. Lucy wasn't a grower —Sam had been that—but she loved to cut and arrange the flowers.

"What's the use now, Reba?"

"Sam didn't like the house without flowers. Remember how he raised Cain till he got the little hothouse, so he could work in it, and you had something in bloom all winter?"

They didn't use the hothouse after his death. Lucy sold it. Reba had said, "But it's worth more than that, Lucy," and she'd replied, "I'd as soon give it away. I don't want to be reminded." And Reba thought of Sam, working in his glass house, with the occasional assistance of the current yardman and sometimes Reba, or of him rushing up to the house yelling, "Come look, girls."

Flowers and plants for winter, and seedlings grown to be set out in the gardens at the proper time by the gardener.

He'd had a passion for lilies of the valley; he had a big bed of them outdoors, and grew them in pots in his hothouse for winter. Reba often picked them, leaning down or squatting. Lucy preferred her roses and other blooms she need not stoop to cut. There were still lilies of the valley outdoors; Sam's original planting had spread. Reba picked them when the reluctant spring coaxed them into bloom. She liked the crisp sound as she pulled them. Lucy, now and then, lent a hand but sometimes pulled too hard and the pip came along with the flower, or she snapped the stems short.

118

The winter following Sam's death Lucy went to Florida but not to any place where she'd been with him. She insisted that Reba come and overrode her objections: "I haven't clothes for the South, just my summer things for here."

"Nonsense," Lucy had said, "I'll buy you some, if you won't do it yourself."

Reba had hated Florida: the tourists, the winter residents, and the transients. She hated brilliant light, the too much sun, the noise around the hotel pool, the widows living on investments and insurance, the elderly retired couples; so many busy, chattering people, like a cageful of bright birds, restless, flitting. She didn't like cocktail parties; she didn't play bridge. Lucy made friends almost immediately; Reba did not. Sitting in the shade near the pool, knitting furiously while Lucy swam, Reba felt alien, as stark and forbidding as her native rocks.

At the end of a month Lucy caught a cold which she couldn't shake and Reba insisted, "I've got to get you back to Pete Harmon." So, the novelty having palled a little, Lucy said all right.

Reba drove their rental car to the airport where they left it and flew to Kennedy to be met by Cynthia and taken back to Westchester for a few cold snowy days. "How you can prefer this to Florida," Lucy exclaimed, "I'll never know." And added, "Sam loved Florida."

It wasn't necessary to love everything Sam had loved, except his cherished dog, the flowers he wanted around him, his wife, his children, his grandchildren, and the smell of his pipe. Sometimes Reba woke from her normal, tranquil sleep and imagined she smelled it there in her quiet room.

After that, Lucy went alone to Florida and left Reba to manage the house, keep it open in case Cynthia or the children wanted to come—usually they didn't—cope with bills, taxes, accounts. Reba kept a meticulous book, using the special checking account Lucy opened for her for wages, repairs, emergencies.

When Reba had come to live with the Pembertons, Sam had wanted to put her on a salary and she'd refused; she wouldn't come on such a basis. "I don't need extra money," she'd told him. "I have my own for personal things and you give me my board and lodging. I've my insurances to bury me, and to see me through any illness."

"Stubborn woman."

"That's right," she had agreed amiably.

She never felt lonely in the house when Sam and Lucy were away together or when Lucy went, alone, to Florida. She had friends, her church, things to look after and people in, the house to ride herd on. Lucy was something of a spendthrift and, for all her being so clever, was easily taken in by so-called friends and people who worked for her. Sometimes Reba thought Lucy wasn't really taken in; she just ignored matters which might prove unpleasant. She'd rather lend or spend more money than necessary than to face a showdown. And she liked to be liked.

Before Sam and Lucy flew to Spain, Sam had spoken to Reba. "Anything can happen on a plane," he told her, in the study.

"For heaven's sake, don't say it," she'd remonstrated. "I don't even like the thought of flying. I'm sure I wouldn't feel at home above the clouds."

Sam had said patiently, "In any case, we've arranged it so you don't have to worry if we go down in a blaze of glory."

"There are worse things," Lucy had interrupted, "because we'd be together."

"Stop sticking your two cents' worth in, Lucy. Anyway, there'll be money to take care of you."

And Lucy had added, "Don't look so grim, Reba, I wouldn't be happy wherever I'd land—on some cloud we flew over, maybe—even with Sam there, if I didn't know you'd be safe for the rest of your life."

"You don't have to do that———"

"Of course not," Lucy agreed, "but we want to, not only because you do so much for us but because we love you."

Reba's throat had hurt; there was an ache behind her eyes, but she'd managed to say, "Well, if you've been that foolish, I hope it's in trust, for Viki and Jenny, after I join you on the cloud." She also managed to smile, sunlight on granite.

"No, I do things my own way," Sam told her. "I'm the Boss. The kids have been looked after; Cynthia too. As far as Lucy and I are concerned you can buy a house, go to Florida, get a handsome husband———"

"God forbid!"

"Take a cruise, take a dozen cruises."

"That wouldn't suit me at all."

"Nonsense," Lucy had said vigorously, "all the new places, sights, sounds———"

"They don't interest me. Plenty of sights and sounds right here in Peaceable."

"I've always yearned to go to Jamaica," Lucy announced dreamily.

"Spain first, woman," said Sam. "After that, Jamaica."

But it had been Spain first and last and never Jamaica.

After Sam's death and the settling of the estate—the house and land were Lucy's; after her, they would be Cynthia's.

Reba went to talk to her banker privately. Could a trust be set up for Viki and Jenny? All she wanted was the income during her life. She'd also asked that any transaction be confidential. She didn't even want the income, but unless she spent something here and there beyond her own means, Lucy would notice and ask questions.

Lucy. . . . Along with this flesh-and-blood legacy,

Reba had inherited Sam's anxiety. She watched Lucy; she knew when she hadn't slept; she knew when she fell into a mood of nostalgia; she knew when grief assailed her. . . . Blunted sorrow can also be a blunt instrument. Reba understood this . . . the blow that comes, waking, sleeping; not sharp, not piercing, but heavy, heavy.

Now she thought: She isn't well; she's going to see Pete.

Lucy had told her so. She'd said, "Next Friday I've a date with Pete."

Reba loved Lucy; she had from almost the moment she'd first seen her. In this house she had observed the relationship between her and Sam. Sometimes it had been amusing. Sam was head of his house; he said so frequently, and believed it. But Lucy always got her way—without tears, nagging, or quarrels. Not that the two didn't quarrel, often in front of Reba, as if she were a familiar piece of furniture or a portrait on the wall—brief, stormy quarrels, always dissolving into laughter.

Lucy could be sharp; Sam knew that. And evasive; he knew that too. Lucy could be as slippery as a cake of wet soap, sliding through your fingers, avoiding capture. Open, candid, honest—that was the outward image.

Reba thought now, in her pleasant room, the windows open to fragrance, bee conversation, bird talk: Is there something the matter, something she hasn't told me?

Lucy. . . . Reba loved her. Reba hated her. Reba had been in love with Sam Pemberton for as long as she could remember. Living here with Sam and Lucy hadn't been easy. It had been, especially when first she'd come, undiluted hell. It had also been heaven, being near and being needed.

11

THE PEMBERTON HOUSE was quiet on that Sunday afternoon. After Mac left and Viki returned to the house, she sat down at her grandfather's desk and wrote a letter. She said, among other things:

You were pretty uptight this morning, not that I blame you. But if the situation bugs you—I mean Mom and Gran's knowing, and eventually Dad—and you want out, tell me so. Have a letter waiting for me at Karen's if you like. I'll still go there no matter what. I promised. You needn't see me. I won't call you from home before I leave. All you have to know is I'll be in Boston sometime Friday.

I can't say I'm not upset by this . . . more because I think you are than anything else. I expect Gran, having thought it over, will consider it her duty to talk to me about it before I leave. She'll hate it, and she won't do well. She wasn't cut out for the lecture platform. Gramp would have raised hell and then—well—sort of consoled me. I've seen him when something Gran did disturbed him.

I'm sorry, Mac, it was my fault. I didn't have to

say anything to Mom. I could have lied myself blue in the face, acted innocent and indignant, and been dishonest. Not that she would have believed me, really, but I've seen enough of parents, mine and other people's, to know that sometimes they'll appear to accept a lie because it's more convenient, on the ignore-it-and-it-will-go-away theory. Unless, of course, there are consequences which can't be ignored. . . .

Anyway, forgive me for getting you into this—I guess I shouldn't have asked you to come to Peaceable. I love you, but don't worry about that. If you'd rather call it all off, remember loving, learning, and losing is a part of growing up—which at times I find unpleasant . . . growing up, I mean.

I'm going out now and climb into the VW, take this to the post office and fling it into the mailbox outside, before I change my mind. Then I'll drive around awhile, maybe even go back to The Park, and come home in time for supper with Gran and Reba. . . . They are both in their rooms now. Sadie's gone out and the house is quiet—like before a cyclone or a hurricane or something. . . .

She rummaged in Sam's desk, found a stamp and went out to her car, which she drove with exaggerated care.

By five o'clock Reba and Lucy had come downstairs and Viki was back in the study, reading. Reba held up the sweater she was knitting for Jenny. She'd made considerable progress.

Lucy said, with astonishment, "I actually went to sleep." Then she asked Viki, "You see Mac off?"

"Yes."

"What have you been doing with yourself all afternoon?" Reba inquired.

"I wrote a letter here, borrowed a stamp too, Gran."

"Help yourself," Lucy said amiably.

"I did, and then I went into the village and mailed it."

"To Mac?" asked Lucy.

"Right on."

Reba asked tartly, "So soon? Isn't that man-chasing?"

"How else you gonna catch 'em?" inquired Viki and Lucy laughed. She thought: I wrote Sam from Aunt Gwen's every day.

Viki said suddenly, "Funny Mom didn't telephone. She must have been home for hours. Mind if I call home?"

"Of course not. But I'm sure your mother's all right," Lucy responded, though she was not at all sure.

Reba said to Lucy, "Cyn's a good driver, keeps her head." She was fond of Cynthia; she respected her for her placid exterior that had started, at least, as a façade but was now part of her. She remembered her as a girl, always so sure of herself. She never sulked, she was never impertinent—as Jenny was now, Reba reflected, but Jenny was another generation. Cynthia and her mother had never been close; as a child it was her father she'd turned to when anything went wrong. She had adored him. Whatever's the matter now, Reba thought, if Sam were here he'd get it ironed out. Cynthia never had real tantrums. Jack had, but almost immediately got over them. Reba's heart ached thinking of Jack. She and Lucy had shared two sorrows from which neither would recover.

Viki, standing by the telephone, reported, "Line's busy, so she's home. No one else is. Jenny's staying at the Owen's, Mrs. Larsen and Edna are off. I don't think they expected Mom back until tomorrow."

Reba got to her feet, saying, "I'll see about supper. Iced tea, iced coffee, or hot?"

Lucy wanted hot tea, Viki wanted iced coffee, and Reba went off to the kitchen where, before coming into the study, she had prepared everything but beverages.

"Maybe you'd rather eat outdoors, early?" she said, returning suddenly.

Lucy said, "I guess not, Reba, unless Viki wants to. . . ."

Viki said, "Gnats and things on the terrace; besides it's starting to cool off."

Reba left again and Lucy asked, "Does it seem to you that Reba has failed? You haven't seen her in quite a while."

"Reba? Heavens, no. She looks just the same to me. I can't even remember when her hair wasn't white."

Viki would have sooner thought of the mountains failing as Reba.

"She was white before you were born," Lucy told her. "I didn't mean her hair, I meant—I don't know—she's always been healthy, but there's something about her—slow, but discernible. She's three years older than I," she added.

"You're a child, Luv," Viki said. "If she hasn't been ill, why are you concerned?" She thought: Gran's the one who's failed—a little. But I suppose they both have, with age.

Lucy thought: Reba's faded, in a way; not that she isn't as strong and capable as ever. . . . It started after Sam died.

She knew all about Reba, her loyalty, her vigorous pursuit of duty, and her love for Sam.

Maybe, she thought now, I should have told Sam I didn't want her in the house—much as I did, actually—but for her sake. I knew long before she came to live with us how she felt about Sam. It was merciless of me to expose her to him day after day, year after year, in order to have the house run, in order not to worry about it or the children, whether we were here or away.

Lucy had thought this often and with guilt, but never by word, glance or gesture, even jokingly, had she suggested to Sam that Reba was in love with him. It would have saddened and deeply embarrassed him, even if he couldn't have believed it; and the fabric of the good affectionate relationship, the long friendship, would have been torn across like a piece of cloth which could never be mended.

Lucy thought: Having Reba come here was, I suppose, the most selfish thing I've ever done. How she must have resented me! But surely whatever Reba had felt—resentment, even hatred—must have been worn down with the years. How had she stood it all that time?

Lucy was sure she knew the answer . . . remembering the fairy story which as a child she had forced herself, crying, to read over and over. The Little Mermaid. She'd thought of it many times watching Reba; but there had been no unguarded moments, except on the day Reba came from Sam's hospital room. Then for the first and only time Lucy had seen her naked face. When Jack died, Reba had wept with his parents, for she had loved him. But when Sam was dying, it was different. The Little Mermaid bleeding, silent, and in pain.

"How come Reba never married?" asked Viki idly.

"I assume because she didn't want to. She had opportunities."

"Was she ever pretty, Gran?"

"No. Always thin, and bones showing; but she had, when I first knew her, lovely heavy hair, going gray even then. And those startling blue eyes, and a fine skin. Craggy, the features. Now and then, when she'd laugh or smile—I remember her playing with your uncle Jack, chasing after him on all fours—she was a lot more than pretty."

"What opportunities did she have?"

"Oh, the minister of her church, after his wife died; and there were others, a farmer—he was a widower too—and a couple of men from Keaton. Her parents' farm was near Keaton and she worked there during the Depression."

"Well," said Viki, yawning from lack of sleep, sun, and the emotional atmosphere of last night and today, "there aren't too many virgins around these days, and haven't been for some time, but I'd bet my glorious hair—my most prized possession—that Reba's one of the few."

"Never speculate on any woman's virginity," her grandmother advised serenely.

"You scandalize me. Are you inferring——"

"For your information the word is not inferring but implying," said Lucy. "I thought you had an English minor."

"Very minor," Viki answered humbly. "All right, have it your way. Are you implying that Reba——"

"Certainly not; it was a generalization."

"Not very tasteful," said Viki who watched Laugh-In, as did her grandmother.

They were both laughing when Reba came to say, "Supper's ready."

Cold lamb, a salad, casserole of hot vegetables, Sadie's home-baked bread, then fruit and cheese . . . hot coffee, iced coffee, hot tea. And Viki said, "That was good, Reba, like wow! I'll help you clear up."

Reba nodded; she believed in the girls helping. "We'll get them rinsed and scraped and into the dishwasher."

Lucy said, "I'll listen to records, look at the news if any, and pour myself a tot of brandy. I don't feel energetic."

"She's just not herself," Reba said worriedly in the kitchen.

Viki sighed. She said, "Gran's tired. There was a family massacre last night."

"What about?"

"Me. Mom was upset. Then she dragged Gran into it."

"I thought something was up when your mother took off this morning. Why, about you?"

"Well, Mac and me."

"Don't tell me about it," said Reba. "It's none of my business."

"But you've suspected the worst?"

"Who's to say what's worse?" asked Reba, practically flinging dishes into the dishwasher. "I don't understand this generation."

"We don't either. Gran will tell you all about it after I go."

"I doubt it."

"She tells you everything." Viki put her arms around the old woman. "You're Family," she added. "And you'd stick by me however much you disapproved."

"I suppose so," Reba admitted.

"And don't worry," Viki told her. "I'm not in what you'd call a 'condition.' "

She went back to the study where Lucy was playing the Irish Rover recordings again.

"I'll try the house once more." Viki said.

The line was still busy.

"Oh, well . . ." Viki murmured. "I'm going to bed if you and Reba don't mind. I'll leave after breakfast, Gran. I may as well face whatever's going on in the jungle."

"Viki, don't say anything to your mother that you'll regret."

"I've already regretted saying what I did last night. If I'd kept my big mouth shut and looked stricken, shocked, and innocent . . ."

"She wouldn't have believed you, dear."

"True. But she would have saved her own face."

At the door, she turned. "Reba has an inkling, but she didn't want it confirmed by me. You'd better tell all after I go," she said.

"Why, in heaven's name?"

Viki said softly, "You have to talk to someone—not

Mom. And Reba can take it." She added after a moment, "I can't help wondering what Mom's up to—unless of course Jenny came home and is on the phone. . . . No, she'd use ours."

When Reba came in, she asked, "Where's Viki?"

"Gone to bed. She's leaving after breakfast. She suspects that you suspect what the excitement was all about last night."

Reba said firmly, "I've eyes in my head, Lucy. I wish it hadn't happened. You'll worry yourself sick."

"And so will you."

"Funny thing! I like that boy," said Reba.

"I do too. Reba, don't get worked up about this. One way or another it will resolve itself. Most things do. I know you're shocked——"

"Nothing really shocks me," Reba said. "I grew up on a farm. I'm just sorry . . . for everybody, especially Viki and Cyn."

After a moment she asked, "Viki ever reach Cyn?"

"No, she gave up finally; no answer."

"That's queer."

"There must be a reasonable explanation, Reba."

"I reckon. . . . What time do you want breakfast?"

"About eight. Viki wants a fairly early start."

Unspoken speculations and anxiety and imaginings rose between them like a chilling, heavy fog and Reba said, "Things change fast. Doesn't seem possible so much has happened since Friday. It started then. Minute I laid eyes on Cyn I knew something was out of kilter. She came here to talk to you about Viki and Mac?"

"No, she didn't even know Mac was coming." Lucy hesitated. "She's having trouble with Edward."

Reba sighed. After a while she said, "I can't say it surprises me."

"Why? It did me—well, not much, perhaps."

Reba said, "I've been around them enough to figure out Edward isn't happy."

"But Cynthia——"

"Cyn's contented enough if she gets her own way," Reba said and thought. She's like you there, except you've always had it. Sam and Edward weren't cut from the same piece of cloth. Aloud, she said, "It's her problem, and Viki's their problem too. No use your fretting yourself. You don't look good, Lucy. I'm glad you're seeing Pete."

"Just a check up."

"But you had one ten days ago."

"He wants to make some tests. Doctors are all alike. If they can't tell you you've acquired some new virus, they want to make tests." She looked up and said in Reba's voice, which was quite unlike her own, "Get along to bed."

Momentarily startled, Reba laughed. Lucy had a gift for mimicry. It had amused Sam, who often remarked that she should be on the stage. He remembered Elsie Janis, singing from the back of a truck in France to thousands of tired cheering soldiers; he had walked a long way in the mud to hear and see her. In the year after their marriage Sam had taken Lucy to New York to meet and hear the sweetheart of the AEF in her concert at Aeolian Hall.

Alone after Reba had gone upstairs, Lucy reflected that the difference between an actress who performed publicly and a woman like herself who performed privately was that the professional knew when she was acting. I don't, Lucy thought; most of us don't. Her most appreciative audience had been Sam, who was quite aware of her ability and entertained by it especially when people came to see them or they went out, and he watched strangers drawn to his wife. He often said, "You turn it on as if it were a faucet."

"I turn what on?"

"The charm," Sam had told her, laughing.

"I know," she'd answered. "Sometimes I'm so charming it nauseates me!"

When she went to bed, she thought: I should have tried to talk to Viki. But she'd avoided it and so had Viki.

Listening to radio recordings of the great old dance bands—this type of music was coming back too—she thought of Eddie Duchin in the Persian Room and tried not to think about tomorrow.

She was almost asleep when the telephone rang, and she sat up, her heart pounding, switched on the light, and picked up the instrument.

"Mother?"

"Wait till I turn off the radio. . . . Are you all right, Cynthia?"

"Yes. Do you know when Viki is coming home?"

"She's leaving here after breakfast tomorrow. She's been trying to call you. We were worried, not hearing."

There was a pause. She heard a man's voice in the background and Cynthia said, "Edward's here," and then he spoke.

"Lucy," he said. He had always called her by her given name, to Cynthia's annoyance.

"How are you, Edward?"

"Okay. I got up here an hour or so ago. You're not to worry; everything's under control."

"You'll see Viki?"

He said carefully, "Presently. I'm returning to town tonight. I'll see her later. Take care . . . go back to sleep."

He hung up. Lucy sat on the edge of her bed, thinking: no reconciliation.

She hadn't expected it. However this was Cynthia's and Edward's personal problem, and sharing concern over a child was not—as a rule—the solution. Life isn't simple, she

132

reflected. Answers aren't in the back of the book or in the crossword section of next day's newspaper. Solutions don't come in neat packages tied with ribbon. If there were to be a mutual future, one of them had to change. Which one would—or could?

Lucy took one of her pills, lay down, switched off the light and ordered herself to hurry into that brief oblivion.

Her last thought before she slept was of Viki. She'd miss her. Viki had her own problem but, thought her grandmother, time would solve it, time and youth.

⟡12

CYNTHIA HAD LEFT early enough on Sunday to miss the traffic until after she stopped for something to eat. She wasn't hungry; she felt sick, but she was empty and a little faint. There were plenty of roadside stands, but she went on to a familiar turnoff where there was a modest restaurant, small, clean and, except for herself and the couple who owned it, unoccupied. She asked, "Am I too early for a pot of coffee and a sandwich?" They said she wasn't.

Fresh coffee was made and a chicken sandwich. She sat next to a window and looked into the green hearts of big trees. Sunshine flickered and birds flew by, talking to one another. It was cool and the owners not inquisitive.

The trip to Peaceable had been a grave mistake. A graver one had been drinking what was, for her, too much; the unaccustomed impact of emotion and alcohol at two in the morning. I was a fool, she thought. And no good had come of it.

The vital thing now was to reach Edward, to demand that he come to Westchester tonight. It was necessary for her to talk to him. He had every right to be informed. He was

134

Viki's father. Their own personal problem must be put aside. That battle could be fought later, and for as long as it took for her to win it. She thought: He's always been lenient with the girls, she thought, as she often did, and Viki's so like him.

When she reached home, no one was there, as she expected. She put her car in the garage, carried her small case to the house, and let herself in. It was warmer here than in Peaceable, the flower fragrance heavier, the smell of the grass, which had been cut the day she left. Friday . . . was it only Friday? But the house was cool, blinds drawn against the sun.

She thought of Jenny and then went to the telephone and called the Owens' house. The maid who answered reported that Miss Jennifer was out riding and Cynthia said, "This is Mrs. Warren. Will you tell her I am home, and ask her to call me when she comes in?"

It would be awkward if Jenny came home this evening, should Edward drive out. But Jenny didn't expect her until tomorrow, Cynthia remembered.

She went into the kitchen and made herself a cup of tea and sat there drinking it. She would have to call his Club, and keep on calling.

She went upstairs and unpacked; she looked into her daughters' empty rooms and shook her head over their customary confusion. If Edna did anything other than dust and vacuum here in the bedrooms and sitting room, Viki and Jenny always restored their living quarters to the usual shambles.

She called the club. Mr. Warren was not in. No he had not left a message where he could be reached. She said, "Will you ask him to call Mrs. Warren, at home, the moment he gets in. This is very urgent."

That went on for a long time: the calls, the same reply, the same message.

She tried to read. She looked blankly at television and turned it off. She made herself eat a small cold supper. She had one drink. She went upstairs again and took a tranquilizer. She put on all the lights so the house blazed. Then she became concerned lest a neighbor stop by, thinking everyone at home. She put them all out except the one over the door, and one in the living room. The telephone rang and she almost ran to it, her heart hammering.

It was Jenny.

"Mom? I couldn't call until we finished dinner; we got in late—Florence, Bo, and I. There was a rock thing going on. We went after we changed from riding. How come you came home today? I thought tomorrow."

"I had things to do."

"Viki there?"

"No, she's staying at Gran's until tomorrow."

"You're alone?"

"Yes, but——"

Jenny said, her voice tinged with instant martyrdom, "If you'd like, I'll come back."

"No. Stay until tomorrow. Isn't that what you'd planned?"

"Sure," said Jenny, radiant with relief. "Florence was talking about a picnic."

"That's all right, dear. Call me tomorrow." She hung up, as relieved as Jenny.

It was nine o'clock before Edward telephoned.

He said, "Cynthia, what's wrong? They gave me half a dozen messages from you, all urgent. I just happened to stop by the Club to change before dinner."

"Dinner? At this hour?"

He said, "I've been out all day, in Bucks county, as it happens. I came back here to change before going out again. What is the matter?"

Bucks county. All day. Dinner at ten, nine-thirty or ten. She said, "Viki . . ."

His voice sharpened. "Is she ill? Has there been an accident?"

"No. She's still at Mother's, and coming home to-morrow. Jenny's at the Owens'. But I have to see you. Viki's in a jam. I must talk to you before you see her. It's vital."

After a moment he said slowly, "I can't imagine. . . . Well, all right. I'll get something quick to eat, make a phone call and come on out."

He replaced the instrument in his room at the Club, then dialed Lisa.

He said, "Darling, I'm sorry, terribly sorry. I can't make it for dinner and the evening. Something's gone wrong at the house. I have to drive out immediately."

She asked in her quick light voice, "Exactly what is wrong?"

"It has to do with one of the girls."

"A trick," she warned him. "A ruse to get you out there and put you through another scene."

"No, I'm sure it isn't."

"You aren't a woman; I'd probably do something similar. But do go, like a good boy scout, prepared." She laughed. "And call me when you get back, no matter what time it is. Even if you never come back, call me to say good-bye."

"Lisa——"

But she had hung up. Angry? Amused? He didn't know. Perhaps he hadn't known her long enough. Perhaps if he knew her until he died, he'd never know. Her unpredictability was, for him, one of her charms. She must use it only in her personal relationships. In her profession she was not temperamental, as far as he knew.

He did not change. He went down to the bar, which

was almost empty, sat against the wall, had a drink, an omelette and coffee, and then walked to the garage, in which he had a short time ago left his car.

One of the attendants said, "I thought you wanted her at nine forty-five. I was just getting ready to bring her around."

"I have to go to the country unexpectedly," he said. "Did you fill her up?"

"Yes, sir."

So he drove out and up to Westchester.

What could have happened? Jam? What kind of jam? Money? Viki had plenty: her own income when she chose to draw upon it, and his allowance. What was there besides money? Drugs? He would not—could not—believe that. They would have known it—at least he would have—from seeing her at home, or perhaps from the Blue Mountain people. From what he'd heard, few institutions were particularly upset unless pupils were on hard drugs, or the less lethal ones caused a bad reaction.

Money, drugs . . . men?

He felt a sharp stab of anxiety and then a dull ache of—what was it—revulsion? But there had been boys flocking around Viki since she was thirteen. She had fallen in and out of love as a child runs down the beach to the sea, puts a bare foot in the water, shivers with joy and a little fear, and then runs back across the wet brown sand, laughing, before a wave can reach her.

He pulled up at his house, and approached it as if he were a stranger. But he had his key, and used it.

Cynthia came from the living room. She said, "You made good time. Did you have something to eat?"

"Enough."

"I've made coffee," she told him, "and of course if you want a drink——"

138

He said impatiently, "I don't want anything. For God's sake, Cynthia, what's this all about?"

She took him into the library. She said quietly, "Please sit down, Edward."

He sat, from custom, at his desk, and she, across from him. She said, "I don't know how to begin."

"At the beginning." He felt himself growing more and more tense. "What has happened to Viki? What has she done?"

"She's become infatuated with a boy in her class . . . he's a little older than Viki."

The tenseness went out of him, like air escaping from a balloon. "That's all! You dragged me up here to tell me that?"

"You don't understand. This is a serious relationship."

"So what? If she's in love, whether she stays in love, or not, she's old enough, Cynthia."

Cynthia said, "She's been sleeping with him, I understand, for all of her junior year." Her composure left her. She put her hands over her face and began to cry.

He said, almost absently, "My poor girl," but she did not know if he meant her or Viki. He asked after a moment, "How did you find out?"

"She told me. He—they call him Mac—came to Peaceable yesterday afternoon. Evidently Viki had arranged it before we left here Friday, although she did ask Mother when he phoned if he might come for dinner and the night. They went for a drive last evening, after dinner, and came back late. I was waiting up for her in her room. And I looked out and saw them come up the stairs and she went in his room. She told Mother, later, it was just to say good night."

"Which it probably was."

He felt a gray desolation. Probably Viki could have been married bell, book and candle and he would have felt the same. Men did when their daughters were bedded; women when their sons took mistresses or brides.

Aloud, he asked, "How did Lucy get into this?"

Cynthia flushed slightly. "She was just next door. And we quarreled, Viki and I . . . anyway, I was so shocked, so horrified, I woke Mother up and had her come in to hear it for herself."

"It would have been kinder to spare her."

"Why? She's my mother. She's Viki's grandmother. I thought perhaps she would try to influence her."

"Whatever gave you that idea? . . . Did she?"

"She didn't attempt to."

After a moment, he said, "Lucy knows a great deal about love."

"We're not talking about love."

"You mean Viki isn't in love with this boy?"

"Oh, she thinks so, I suppose. But it's simply sex."

"Lucy knows a good deal about that too."

Cynthia looked at him. Her eyes were as blue as the Mediterranean, as cold as the Antarctic Ocean and as hard as marble.

"We aren't here to discuss my mother."

"I suppose not. . . . Who is he?"

"His name is McDonald," said Cynthia. "I forget his first name. It doesn't matter. He's nobody."

"Viki evidently doesn't agree with that. Where's he from?"

"Boston. And that," said Cynthia loudly, "is where he'll be working this summer and where Viki is going to work. She leaves Friday. For the whole summer, before their senior year."

"Will they be living together?"

"No. She's going to stay with some girl in her class. Karen something or other, who has an apartment."

140

He wasn't listening now. He asked, half fearfully, as he didn't really want to know and, half aggressively, because he was curious, "What's he like?"

"What does it matter? He has a physical attraction."

"You say physical, you mean animal. In other words a normal, healthy young man."

She said sharply, "What are you going to do about this?"

"Nothing," said Edward.

She rose so abruptly that the small chair in which she'd been sitting toppled and fell. He made no move to rise and recover it. She stood with her hands flat on the desk. "You're her father, and you won't do anything?" she asked.

He said, "Cynthia, it's been a long time since fathers threw daughters into the snow." He frowned. "She's not pregnant?"

"No. In this era you apparently don't have to be."

He said, "Well, that's good. Cynthia, she'll be twenty-one before she graduates next year. She has her own money, in case you're thinking I'll cut off her allowance. This is her show; it's not ours."

"What kind of a father are you?"

"I'd hoped, a good one," he answered. "One, anyway, willing to go with my daughter every step of the way."

"I'll never understand you!"

"No."

She walked away and stood by the mantelpiece. "I might have known," she said slowly, "how it would be with Viki. She's very like you."

"Oh, so that's it? . . . Possibly. I've wondered a little myself. I'm sorry—which is an inadequate word—that this has happened. I'd rather see her safely married, of course. Is she by any chance considering that?"

"No. She would have said so."

"I see."

"She'll be home sometime tomorrow. I'll expect you here to talk with her. I'll call Mother now and ask when Viki's leaving."

"I'm going back to town. I'm not coming out tomorrow. I'll probably hear from Viki. In any case, after she goes to Boston, I'll see her—alone."

She asked, her voice shaking with anger, "And the boy?"

"I don't know. Actually, I'd rather not. But I shall if Viki wants me to. I'm damned sure he'd rather not, also," he added.

She said, "You're a coward, Edward."

"That's possible," he agreed. He looked very tired. He added, "I will not have a crying, shouting, encounter between you, Viki, and myself. I'll see her alone, and when she wants to see me. I have no intention of losing her, Cynthia. I love her very much."

"You're saying that I don't?"

"Oh, in your way," he said wearily, "in your way."

She said bitterly, "This has been a wonderful weekend—first you, then Viki."

"Weekends don't last forever."

"Consequences do. If you think I'll give you a divorce, you're out of your mind; and if you try to get one, I'll contest it."

"Of course. Did you tell Lucy about us?"

"Yes."

"And what was her advice?"

"It was hardly advice," Cynthia said.

"I suppose not." To her astonishment, he laughed. He said, "I know your mother better than you do; and I like her a great deal more. Lucy never makes proclamations; in all the time I've known her, she hasn't made decisions. At least, never appeared to. Your father made them for her which is the way she wanted it, as he always almost always made them her way. Now, I daresay, Reba, in another fashion does . . . what to wear, what to eat——"

"If my father were here——"

"But he's not." He rose. He said, "Tell Viki to write me, if and when she wants to, and that I'd like to come to Boston to see her, also if and when——"

She said—and now she was crying again—"You're not coming back here?"

"Yes, to see Jenny, when things quiet down."

She said dully, the tears on her cheeks, "I thought you'd tire of this—this——"

"I don't think so, Cynthia, but I don't know. There are times when I believe I'm tired of everything, especially women. This doesn't happen to be one of them——"

She said, "I'm going to call Mother and find out when Viki's starting for home; I insist that you see her. You owe me that much. And Viki—much as she'll hate the situation—she'll find it incredible that you don't want, even demand, a meeting. She'll think you don't care about her."

"All right," he said, "call your mother. Tell her I'm here. I'll speak to her."

"What for?"

"She'd expect it. I won't see Viki here with you. Tell her when she gets home to telephone me at the office tomorrow. She can come in and see me there."

Cynthia went to the telephone and he said, "Control yourself. There's no use upsetting Lucy more than she's upset already."

"What makes you think she's upset?"

She made the call. Edward had his brief conversation, hung up and went to the door. Cynthia followed him. He said, standing there, "I'll be in town. I was going to write you to

143

say I'm depositing sufficient funds to your account tomorrow, and shall, every month. So you can keep up this place until you decide what you want to do."

She said a little wildly, "Do? I want things to be as they were before!"

"Things haven't been the same for a long time and they never will be. Perhaps one of us could change. I doubt if you can. I don't know. At the moment, I'd say I can't either. In any case it won't be the same for Viki, or with Viki. Make up your mind to accept that."

"What am I to tell Jenny? She probably heard us quarreling."

"Tell Jenny the truth; that we have separated. You needn't go further than that with her now."

She put her arms around him suddenly and held fast. "I can't let you go," she said.

"Actually you did years ago." He disengaged himself gently, touched her hair briefly. He said, "I'm sorry. You were such a pretty girl, Cynthia, and I loved you so much."

He went out; the door closed; she heard the car start and drive away, and stood there, not crying now—alone in an empty house.

∾13

EDWARD DROVE BACK to the city with unusual care. His official driving record was close to flawless: in all his motoring life, three tickets; one years ago, in upstate New York, for speeding; two for jumping lights.

Now, leaving his house, a symbol of his success, he wished he'd never see it again, but he would, of course, however things went. He had reached an age—which can be any age from seven to seventy—when the male yearns for a beach and palm trees, and no Friday, either girl nor man . . . when he desires passionately to leave parents, wife, children, grandchildren and sail the seven seas, or take a walking trip through rural England or France or Africa, anywhere where there are no responsibilities, no crises. The heroes of a great many novels have done this—blithe, unencumbered, using other names—painting, seafaring, occasionally working in some obscure village, but always free . . . at least, for the time being.

Other men, nonfictional, have often escaped the routine and the commuting train by voluntarily going off to wars. Many have been killed. A few are found years later, living in other countries with other wives and children. All have found in the services another routine, but less responsibility, for over the privates are the NCOs and over the NCOs the commissioned officers, and over each officer, another of higher rank. So it's not often that the escapee need make decisions. And those who do return must come back to decision-making, the commuter train, the subway, or the car.

Edward was, by now, overage for the current disasters; he'd had his war, which he had for the most part rather enjoyed.

Thinking of Viki was a knife in his gut. It was sorrow, pain, and regret; it was also anger, not directed at her, not even particularly directed at a young man he now thought might be the likable one he had met just once at the Christmas season, but at everything—living, loving, and helpless involvement.

Thinking of Cynthia was a small rodent nibbling at his mind, biting sharply into the stuff of memories, good, bad and indifferent; perhaps the indifferent memories were the most hurting. How does it begin and why, the journey from love, hope, and desire to disillusion?

Thinking of Lisa was like remembering a book in which you had read just a few pages; but a book in which, anxious to learn the ending, you could not turn the unread pages to the last one and there, prematurely, learn the denouement, and satisfied begin where you left off, or dissatisfied, close the book forever.

With his physical eyes on the road and the signs, his reactions excellent, his hands, his foot obeying him, his thoughts saw, heard, and remembered.

He had not been astonished, in Jamaica, to find himself momentarily responsive to a pretty woman on the beach, on the streets, in the hotel lounge, at a nearby table under the stars. He'd been responsive to pretty women since he was, perhaps, fourteen. The careless glance, the shoulder-shrugging

146

admission of a familiar reflex, did not disturb him. He had been, for the first time in his life, deeply in love and wholly committed, which rarely means that one cannot admire without wishing to possess. Pretty women were as objets d'art, paintings, shadows on a screen, figures in landscapes, beauty on a stage. Cynthia was alive, she was reality, and she belonged to him, from, he had thought, the first moment he saw her at the crowded noisy cocktail party where, going up in an elevator, he'd regretted he'd accepted and, having accepted, wondered why had he come. One man less would make no difference. Also the party was for the daughter of the house, just out of college, and the guests would consist mainly of her contemporaries, male and female. He felt centuries older. He wasn't, of course, but college was behind him, also a war, and he was earnestly engaged in achieving some stature in his uncle's business. The reason he'd received this invitation was simple enough: extra men are always invited everywhere because they enhance the scene, particularly eligible men. His reason for accepting was just as simple. His host, the girl's father, was a valuable client of the advertising agency.

Then, as bored as he'd expected to be, he'd seen Cynthia.

It was a good merger, practically speaking: excellent families and social backgrounds—the Pembertons and the Warrens. Also money: the Pemberton Mills, and the successful agency. And from the less practical viewpoint a handsome young man and a handsome younger woman; in short, a suitable couple.

But he had no such motives, he merely fell in love and was swept out to sea on a wave of physical attraction stronger than any he'd ever felt; and swimming sure, determined, the currents didn't matter, or the tides, or even if perhaps he died by drowning.

In a way, he had.

There was no family disapproval, from his mother or Cynthia's parents. He wouldn't have cared had there been and he didn't think of asking Cynthia how she would have felt, had there been family dissension. Why should he? Cynthia was of age; he could support her; no one could stop them from marrying. His mother was not given to sudden enthusiasms; she had to know people for some time before she loved them, but she'd liked Cynthia, who was deferential, and who had good manners as well as beauty. As for the Pembertons, Edward fell in love with them too, with Lucy, and with Sam, a very satisfactory comrade. *cum* father image. Edward scarcely remembered his own father, and his uncle had never been a satisfactory substitute. He was devoted to his mother, and she to him, but she was not demonstrative; she was somewhat shy and withdrawn. He'd never been able to fathom her; he knew nothing about her except what she permitted him to see: the valid but unspoken affection, generosity and interest; her quiet intelligence and serenity which might or might not have been a mask such as actors hid behind, in the old Greek tragedies, and some of the modern dramas. He'd no idea what her relationship had been with his father. He had known as a child that she grieved but without breast-beating or outcry. He heard her talk of her husband, not very often, all the brief rest of her life with affectionate praise. Cynthia had been fond of her; that much he knew. How Mrs. Warren felt toward Cynthia, other than approval, he never knew.

Years after his marriage, he'd wondered if there wasn't something after all in the theory of the search for the mother in the wife—not that he had been overattached to his mother. Cynthia, however, had some of her qualities; she was more robust, and handsomer by far, although Mrs. Warren had possessed a delicate elegance. But Cynthia had, or so he had believed, the quiet intelligence and the serenity. At first her lack of valid physical response had not too much disturbed him. He respected and also took a delight in her inexperience and shyness; even her withdrawals from him were not at first an affliction. Perhaps again, this was a reflection of his mother? In any case, he was the teacher and Cynthia the pupil, and everything would resolve itself happily . . . given time, patience, and consideration.

It hadn't done so.

It was some years thereafter he came to the wretched conclusion that the teacher had failed, and the pupil would be forever a lovely dropout that had triggered the first of a few unimportant casual episodes about which Cynthia knew nothing. Then nine years ago the girl in the office, the pretty, stupid wide-eyed girl who used the telephone one night. That, he reflected, was when it really hit the fan.

It was, of course, guilt and feeling no commitment to the girl. She meant nothing to him, apart from pleasure and a consoled vanity. The realization of what would happen if his uncle learned of his indiscretion—for the old man had still been alive nine years ago, and keeping a sharp eye on the business—sent Edward home again, after an affair which had lasted two weeks. Prior to that, a few cautious meetings at lunch or dinner had preceded the longer evenings in her rather vulgar little flat from which fortuitously a roommate had departed.

As for the rest of the nine years, now and then a casual indulgence, rather like a handshake—hello, good-bye —until Lisa.

Lisa had also come to him through the office, if in a very different capacity. She worked, rewardingly, for a well-known successful fashion magazine which employed the advertising agency. Office meetings, lunches, dinners, and finally another apartment. This one was spacious and beautiful. The decor in excellent taste, understated, and costly. Lisa lived alone, and had for some time. She'd had one brief disastrous marriage when she was eighteen. There had been no children for which, she said, she thanked God. But she was young enough to bear a child and now she wanted one very much, perhaps two . . . and soon. She was thirty-two and sick of what she rather quaintly called "passing fancies." Edward had not asked details: when, how many, name, age, serial number? He had understood from the beginning—rumor, scuttlebutt and warnings—that Lisa conducted her life as she saw fit.

She was, of course, interested in Women's Lib. She too had no wish to be merely a sex symbol, she said, although heaven knew she was, he'd thought, during their first personal discussion—nor to be a kitchen slave. Actually she was a gourmet cook when she wanted to be, which recently had been quite frequently. With her well-paid job she could afford a maid, but there was always cook's night out. And she hadn't, she said later, the courage to have a child outside the gates as it were, as some of her friends had done, earnestly protesting their right to procreation without any assistance other than the necessary biological help. "Besides," said Lisa dreamily, "it isn't fair to a child, not really."

Lisa had reached an age also—and this, in women, is any age from eleven to seventy-five or eighty years—when she wanted, above all things, security, love, companionship.

Unpredictable she was, even in her desire to build a new house, acquire a new name, start a family. He'd been completely astonished when she had said flatly, "You must ask for a divorce, darling."

He'd said, troubled, "Cynthia won't divorce me, Lisa; she's adamantly opposed to divorce."

"On religious grounds?" she'd asked, startled.

"No. She doesn't believe in it, but she comes of a long line of people who stay married, no matter what." As I do, he thought.

"You can divorce her then."

"She'd fight it."

"Let her," Lisa advised magnificently.

There were later discussions, questions, answers . . . no recriminations, however, no scenes.

"Have you spoken to Cynthia yet?"

"No."

"Why not?" He remembered she had risen and moved across the living room restlessly, looked from the windows to the East River, sighed, and turned to face him.

"I'm scared," he admitted.

She'd laughed, and returned to herself; light, lithe, fragrant—her perfume was like the apartment, understated and expensive—and she'd said, "You'll get over it," adding, more soberly, "Or—God forbid—over me. I won't nag you. I promise I'll wait, but not too long. I can't wait five or eight or ten years. I can't waste my time or yours, no matter how much I love you, and you, perhaps, me."

"No perhaps about it, Lisa."

He had spoken at another time of hard, practical facts. "I'm not making as much as I did once, Lisa; you know that; it's true of everyone. Your outfit, for instance, is cutting down."

"On advertising yes, and some of the lesser menials."

"Some not as lesser, if one is to believe so-called resignations as well as out-and-out firing."

"But they can't get along without me," she'd said. "And I can't get along without you. . . . Oh, I suppose I could, after a while. There are always substitutes," she warned carelessly, "but I wouldn't like it—or them."

He was disturbed by imagination. He'd tried always to shut out the "passing fancies" from his mind. Now his mind painted very graphic pictures of substitutions.

"About money . . . I've never saved much; most of my

stocks are, of course, down. And I've an expensive household, including two daughters. Cynthia would demand and get a settlement and support," he said.

"I thought she had her own income."

"She has; and the girls have too. Viki already, Jenny pretty soon, but it isn't enough; she'd never have enough."

"So she's greedy!"

"No, she isn't. But it would be one way of expressing her resentment. It's no use, Lisa. Even if Cynthia would divorce me, she'd demand the girls."

"But they're grown up, or almost. You told me Viki's twenty and Jenny ready for college. You'd have access to them through the courts, and besides they're old enough to make up their own minds. You'd see them; they'd visit us." She didn't say, "And eventually live with us." He didn't think of that until afterwards.

She told him after a moment, "I've saved, Edward, and I can go on working. I could get a leave of absence when I had a baby, and afterwards go back to work." She'd added, as an afterthought, that she owned stock in the magazine, a fact she'd omitted to mention until then. It was good strong stock; it was also expensive. The yield wasn't great, but the stock was.

"How'd you ever afford it?"

And she answered, "Oh, I bought a little, and was given the rest."

A passing fancy? The old man who'd owned the majority of the stock, Edward remembered, had retired as Chairman of the Board a few years ago, and then died.

He'd felt at that moment a strong, nauseating revulsion, but immediately Lisa was in his arms, saying, "Don't look so grim, darling; it will all work out."

Last Thursday night he'd finally found the courage;

he had been swept into another sea, this one of boiling anger, frustration and boredom; last Friday morning he had driven to town and his Club and called Lisa.

She'd said, "How wonderful! No matter what she does you've made the break . . . and we can plan our future." She was crying she said, with a catch in her voice, from "sheer completely marvelous happiness."

Now it was Sunday and he'd gone back to West-chester and was returning to his Club, and Lisa. He'd promised to call her.

There is no spiritual or mental blender which can smoothly, mechanically, mix conflicting emotions and manufacture something nourishing to soul and body.

He was so damned sorry for Cynthia because of what she was. Presumably the fault was not entirely hers. Someone, somewhere in her background, had handed her a particular legacy; not Sam, not Lucy. He remembered Lucy speaking of Sam's mother, after his death. "Difficult," she'd said, "domineering; she frightened me sometimes." She had not said, "Cynthia's a little like her." Lucy didn't often speak bluntly; Lucy implied, her voice trailing off, a sentence left unfinished.

So perhaps it was Cynthia's paternal grandmother, perhaps her individual self, perhaps himself, or a mixture of these . . . but he had to be sorry for her. He hadn't been when she had screamed and wept and called him names he hadn't known she'd ever thought of . . . but he was sorry for her now, having seen her broken, through Viki.

Cynthia, Lisa, Viki . . .

"God damn it," he said aloud.

He was very tired. And tomorrow Viki would telephone him, or the next day. Tonight, he'd call Lisa. He had no wish to discuss Viki with her; he would not. He had never, except in simplest terms, discussed Cynthia with her; he'd merely said he no longer loved her, they were not compatible. He had said further that she would not give him a divorce. He'd still have to say that.

It was very late when he reached his room in the Club. He picked up the telephone, and after a while Lisa answered sleepily.

"Oh, darling, I've been walking the floor, waiting . . . and then I came to bed and must have fallen asleep. Is everything all right? Viki, I mean."

He said, "It's nothing to worry about—a misunderstanding between her and her mother. I'll straighten it out."

"You sound so tired."

"I am, and I have appointments tomorrow."

She knew better than to ask then: And what about Cynthia? What about the divorce? She said, "Go to bed, poor baby. . . . I'll see you tomorrow night."

～14

AFTER BREAKFAST MONDAY, Viki went upstairs to strip her bed and look around the room to see if she'd left anything out of the tote bag. She usually did and Reba would mail it to her, a postal arriving in advance saying, "I'm sending your pajamas"—or whatever the article was. "Wish you could have stayed longer, but then you might have left more. Love, Reba." And Viki would tell her parents, or Jenny, or anyone who happened to be around, "I left something at Gran's again. Here's a card from Reba, and even the ink looks resigned."

No. This time she'd left nothing material, but she'd lost something valuable. She wasn't sure what it was. Not Mac, not for a while anyway, she thought. Not Gran. But there was a hollow place within her, an empty spot which hadn't been there before.

As she went downstairs, she heard Reba busy in the kitchen, the water running.

"Gran?"

"She's in the study," Reba told her, appearing. "I've got something for you to take along with you, so don't go kiting off without it. And drive carefully; it's raining hard."

"When did it start?"

"Around four o'clock, a little thunder, a little lightning, then it steadied down. We need the rain."

Viki said, "I've time to help with the dishes."

"No need. Go say good-bye to your grandmother."

Viki went to the study where Lucy was writing a letter. She said, looking up, "I wish you could stay on."

"Me too, but better not." She came in and sat down, and Lucy thought: The bounce has gone out of her, the elasticity. Aloud, she said, "Too bad it's raining—the driving's harder."

"I don't mind. Actually, I'm glad. I've always hated to leave Peaceable when the sun's shining and the gardens bright." She smiled briefly. "Suits my mood, today, especially."

"I think you're scared, Viki."

"Of what? Oh, Mom, you mean."

"Not particularly; nor your father—just the situation."

"I guess so," Viki said slowly. "Everything's changed, since Friday . . . Thursday night, really."

"Changes come every day," Lucy commented, "only we don't see them. No one's the same person today that he was yesterday."

"I feel as if I'd lost something."

"What?"

"I don't know, really. It seems silly to say this—freedom, maybe. No—feeling free. There's a difference."

"Your privacy perhaps," Lucy told her, "or what you thought of as your privacy. And you feel responsible for whatever has happened or will happen. It's a part of growing up." She looked at Viki thoughtfully, and added after a moment, "I don't speak exactly from experience, but rather observation."

Viki said soberly, "I can't feel penitent, Gran, except about the scene with Mom and you being dragged in it."

"No. As I reminded you—was it Saturday night?—just being found out upset you, which isn't remorse."

"Could be. I'm pretty mixed up at the moment."

"You'll get things sorted out. Better get started, Viki. Call me when you're home."

"Of course." Lucy got to her feet and Viki rose and hugged her hard. She said, "Take care of yourself, Gran."

"I shall; it's a bore, but I promise. Give my love to Jenny. I'd wish she'd come up."

"Maybe Mom will bring her one weekend. Jenny's talking about doing hospital work as a candy striper."

"That's good. If—when—you see your father, give him my love too, and remember me to Mac."

"Poor Gran," said Viki, with compunction. "You've had a lousy weekend, thanks to me—and Mom."

"It hasn't been exactly fun and games," Lucy admitted, "but I daresay that's family life."

"I'm sorry. People ought to be like wild animals."

"They are," said Lucy, "sometimes."

"I mean, once the bird can fly, throw it out of the nest; teach the cub to fend for himself and kick him out of the den or wherever. I bet animals wouldn't even know their own kids if they met them later, unexpectedly, to say nothing of the grandchildren they'd never seen; and that goes for the birds and the bees."

She went to the door and Lucy said, "Drive carefully," and Viki promised, "I shall" and neither said goodbye. Viki said, "See you, Gran," and went out into the hall where Reba was waiting. She had a square bright-colored cooler in her hands.

"What's that?"

"Lunch. These roadside places can be instant ptomaine. I thought you could pull off into a rest area and have a picnic. If it keeps on raining, you can eat in the car. If it clears along the way, then get out and stretch your legs."

Viki put her arms about her. She said. "Thanks, Reba. What's in that gas jet?"

"Thermos of iced tea, sandwiches, fruit. Saw this at Simpkins the other day, and bought it. I hadn't the least idea why. Lucy and I don't go on picnics; and besides this isn't big enough for two. Take it back to school with you. I had the yard boy"—she snorted slightly—"that's George. You haven't seen him yet; he's fifty if he's a day. . . . Anyway, I had him bring your car around. Stop for gas at Dan's."

"The VW doesn't drink much."

Reba said, "Stop just the same and mind you don't skip lunch."

"Okay, Reba. I forgot to give Gran my summer-job address. I'll send it. Both of you write me, please."

She went out to the door, and Reba did not follow. She looked in at the study and reported, "Viki's off."

"I know. I heard."

They stood there together, silent, two old women, and heard Viki speak to George, and heard the car start.

"That's that," said Reba. "I'll get back to the kitchen."

"What for? Breakfast dishes for three? I suppose you noticed Viki ate scarcely anything. Just coffee, crumpled up her toast and she didn't want eggs. Reminded me of her mother. Cynthia always starved herself when she was upset. Luckily it never lasted long."

"Well, I must say, I don't envy Viki going back to face——"

"If you say 'the music,' I'll scream!"

"The music," Reba concluded calmly, "and scream your head off. It's very quiet round here all of a sudden. Sort of pleasant after the last few days. And there's no one to hear you except George and the roses; and George is a little hard of hearing. How do you think he's working out?"

"George is all right and he isn't really deaf you know, except to orders of which he doesn't approve. Gardeners are natural dictators—or maybe rebels. How long has he been here anyway?"

"January. I hired him when old Yates retired, and you were in Florida."

"Seems incredible Viki hasn't been here since Yates left."

"Everything's incredible. . . . Sadie should be home pretty soon. Any plans?"

"Just to finish the mail, take a walk, perhaps drive to the village before lunch, or cut a few flowers, or both. We're due at Nellie Howard's for tea, remember?"

"Can't I get out of it?"

"No. You're almost as old a friend of hers as I am."

"Weak tea, hot or cold," predicted Reba sadly, "and a long recital about how Peacable's grown, and all the motor-cycles, the summer visitors and what she's knitting, and her grandchildren."

Lucy gave her a brief affectionate shove. She said, "Run along and polish the kitchen to shame poor Sadie. You'll live through Nellie's repetitions. What else has she to talk about?"

"The stock market and politics, local and national."

"I daresay that women of our age aren't particularly exciting conversationalists."

"That's right," Reba agreed. "Sometimes when I talk to myself, I get bored. . . . Lucy, don't worry too much about Viki."

"I won't, if you don't."

"We both will," said Reba. "Looks as if it might clear

159

in a few hours, and she could stop and get out of that kiddie car and enjoy her lunch somewhere."

IT HAD CLEARED by the time Viki felt a healthy desire for nourishment. The rest area had tables and shade and, except for herself, was deserted. She drank her tea, ate her sandwiches and fruit, and watched the cars go by. Now and then one slowed down tentatively, driven by a lone male who saw her sitting there, the copper hair dappled by sunlight. Then, receiving not the least encouragement, mindful that he had a man to meet by appointment, or something to sell if lucky, he drove on.

When Viki left, she did not hurry. She wished the drive would last forever. Well—almost forever. The traffic was light until she was nearing home. When she drove up, Maisie was barking at the door, Jenny flew out, and Mrs. Larsen was close behind her.

"Good trip, Miss Viki? Everyone well?"

"Fine. Is Mother home?"

"She's in her room," said Jenny. "I had the most divine time at Florence's. They want me to go to the Cape with them for a week or ten days. Mom says forget it. I could kill myself. Viki, you persuade her to let me go."

"I thought you were going to work!"

"I am. There's plenty of time. I can be a candy striper or work in the gift shop. Candy striper is more interesting and besides in the shop I'd have to make change and math has never been my best subject."

"I know. It's a miracle you got into Blue Mountain."

As they went into the house, Mrs. Larsen vanished kitchenward, saying, "It's roast lamb," and Viki and Jenny smiled.

"Nothing on her mind but what's for dinner," Jenny said, Maisie running ahead of them.

"About Blue Mountain," Jenny went on complacently. "Nowadays it's more important to have personality than straight A's . . . also extracurricular activities."

"Depends on what they are."

"I play a mean game of tennis, swim, scuba dive."

"In a pool?"

"Well—I swim anyway. My guitar isn't bad. I can sing, and I've been class president twice at Country Day."

"Spare me your credits. . . . Gran and Rebe sent love."

"How are they?"

"All right. They'd like to see you. I thought Mom could take you up for a weekend before school starts."

"Groovy idea. I might even go on my own, of course, with permission, and someone who rates a car. But I do want to go to the Cape. When Dad gets home, I'll work on him. He's more reasonable. Where is he anyway, in Tibet? Mom just says, 'business.' Are the llamas advertising this year?"

"I don't know where he is, Jenny."

"For heaven's sake . . ." Jenny began, but Viki was halfway up the stairs. She said over her shoulder, "I promised I'd call Gran; come along and speak to her." She tossed her tote and handbag on her bed and went into their living room-study, and dialed. Jenny came in, and Maisie barked; she was fascinated by telephones.

"Gran? . . . Yes, the trip was all right. Tell Reba it cleared and I ate lunch outdoors. It was great. . . . I'll send you my summer address. . . . Jenny wants to say hello. Thanks again and love to you both."

Jenny was talking when Viki went down the hall to their mother's room. Cynthia was standing idly by the windows looking out, as if watching for someone. But not for me, thought Viki, plagued by pity and exasperation.

Viki thought: Sister Anne. But this was not the time

to say it. Instead, she said unnecessarily, "Mom, I'm home."

"Yes, I saw you drive up," Cynthia said, turning. She wore her favorite face, composed, beautifully made up. "I expected you much earlier."

"I took a little longer than usual."

"I thought you had." She crossed over to the door and closed it. "Sit down," she said. "I have something to tell you before you change for dinner."

Viki did so obediently and Cynthia, perched on the end of the chaise, said, "I sent for your father last night."

Viki felt sick. She swallowed, and then asked evenly, "Did he come?"

"Of course, once I'd convinced him how serious it is."

"And?"

"He wants to see you."

Oh, no he doesn't, thought Viki. You want him to see me.

Aloud she asked, "Here?"

"No. He said he'd rather see you in New York. He wants you to call him at the office. I was hoping you'd be home early enough to do just that, before he leaves."

"I'll call him tomorrow," Viki said.

"Very well. I know it will be unpleasant for you both. But you're both old enough, I hope, to understand that it is vital. I called your grandmother while he was here to see when you'd planned to start home today and your father spoke with her."

Viki said, trying to sound indifferent, "About me?"

"Of course not."

"Gran didn't tell me she'd spoken to him."

"I didn't expect her to," said Cynthia. "After he left here I made up my mind that I would have no more discussions with you about your behavior at Peaceable, and before that. I've said all I have to say. And the last thing I want is

162

to have Jenny overhearing. I don't suppose that everyone at Blue Mountain is ignorant of the situation—and I wish she weren't going there."

"Why? Because you consider me a bad example?"

"Do you think of yourself as a good one? Jenny is younger. She looks up to you and worships you."

"Jenny's concerned only with herself," said Viki sharply. "She's fond of me, yes, when she isn't mad at me." And she added, "I think she feels pretty much the same about you. . . . Not Dad, she's really hooked there."

Cynthia said, expressionless, "You both are."

"What reason did you give her for not letting her go to the Cape with Florence?"

Cynthia lifted an eyebrow. "I merely told her I didn't wish her to go."

"That's not enough," said Viki. "And what is the reason?"

"I expect her to do something useful this summer."

"She still can; she was asked only for ten days."

Cynthia said after a moment, "You're going to Boston, and you and Jenny will both be in college in the autumn. Am I supposed to stay here alone?"

"Jenny deserves a reason—not just 'no' and that's that. She's outgrown commands; she's seventeen. Why don't you tell her the truth?"

"I intend to," said Cynthia after a moment. She hadn't. Edward had said, "Tell her the truth." Now Viki. If Cynthia didn't, they would. It would be comforting, she thought drearily, to have one ally in this miserable divided house.

Viki said with an effort, "I'm sorry, Mom. About everything."

"So am I. It doesn't help. Do get ready for dinner."

When Viki returned to her room, Jenny was there, the recorder was going in their living room . . . someone

163

singing, "I don't want to leave him now," and Viki said, "Turn that thing off."

"Okay. Did you ask Mom about the Cape?"

"I did. Negative."

"Hell," said Jenny. Maisie, lying in a corner, looked at her with large reproachful eyes. Maisie knew something was going to happen which she wouldn't like . . . not right away but soon enough. "Well, perhaps you'd take me to the hospital. I'll make a date with Mrs. Parsons. Like tomorrow or Wednesday," Jenny suggested.

"We'll see. I may have to go to town Wednesday."

"New York?" asked Jenny aghast. "What for? Oh— Mac maybe?"

"He's in Boston."

"The plot thickens," said Jenny.

"Keep on reading," Viki advised, "and do something about your hair. Dinner will be ready anytime now."

15

CYNTHIA HAD A DRINK before dinner; just one. She felt
Viki's regard and looked away. She'd been a fool at Peaceable.
Drinking herself into an unusual sodden stupid condition
which resulted only in embarrassment and a hangover. And
Viki would report it to Edward. No, she wouldn't, thought
Cynthia, she's not a tale bearer.

Viki took a splash of vodka and tomato juice. She
didn't often, and she didn't really want it, but she couldn't let
Cynthia drink alone, sitting there, elegant and grim.

"Bunch of alcoholics," commented Jenny cheerfully.
"I'm never going to drink—at least I don't think so," she added
honestly.

"Good for you," Viki said.

"When I make up my mind to do something, I do it.
Mom, won't you change your mind, about the Cape?"

"No, Jennifer."

When anyone in the family called her Jennifer, Jenny
knew she was licked. She said, "You might at least tell me
why?"

"I'll tell you after dinner," Cynthia said. Viki started,
and set her glass down carefully.

Dinner was excellent, as usual, and Jenny was starved. She said happily, "I eat like a horse."

"Watch it," suggested Viki. "Even horses get fat."

"I do watch it. Maybe it's just as well I'm not going to the Cape—all those lovely clams and lobsters and oceans of butter."

Viki, to her astonishment, was also hungry. She spoke of the lunch Reba had packed for her. "That Reba!" said Jenny. "She thinks of everything. Mom, can't we go up some weekend?"

"Of course, if your grandmother will have us."

"She loves having us," Jenny said. "Well, that's something to look forward to. I adore Peaceable."

After dinner, coffee. Mrs. Larsen poured and departed. And Jenny asked, "So okay, Mom, why can't I go to the Cape?"

Cynthia said firmly, "Because I want you with me. Viki's going to Boston on Friday. She'll just be back briefly before she's off to Blue Mountain. You'll be going somewhat ahead of her. It won't be so bad, Jenny," she added, trying to smile, "you'll have your friends here."

"Most of them go away."

"Not all, I'm sure. And Florence will be back in—what did you say—ten days? You'll have your work at the hospital; you can ride; have people here. We'll go to the Club for dinner now and again, and there are the weekends." She hesitated, and said slowly, "I don't want to be here alone."

Viki's throat tightened. This wasn't an act. Cynthia wasn't given to performances. Oh, one woman on the surface, another beneath it—but when she spoke as she had just now, she meant it.

"But Dad will be here," Jenny argued.

Cynthia put down her cup. Viki held her breath and then their mother said, "No, Jenny, your father and I have

166

separated. And, as I've told Viki, one of you must stay with me this summer. Viki can't or won't, so it's up to you."

Jenny looked at her sister, "You didn't tell me," she said outraged. "You knew about Dad and you didn't tell me!"

"It isn't my ball game, Jenny."

Cynthia said, "I asked Viki not to."

"It's Dad you're going to see in New York?"

"I'm to call him tomorrow," Viki told her.

"Why can't I go with you? He's my father too."

Cynthia said patiently, "Your father and Viki have something to discuss. You'll see him Jenny, in town or here, I promise."

"You both make me sick," Jenny said violently. "I'm not a child." She came to her feet, overturned a cup, and ran from the room in tears.

Cynthia rose, but Viki said, "Better leave her alone for a while, Mom. I'll go up and talk to her presently."

"I knew this would happen," Cynthia said, "when your father and then you insisted that I tell her."

"You could hardly keep it a secret," Viki reminded her.

"When you see him, tell him he must see her."

"I will; he will. It will all work out."

"Nothing's working out," Cynthia said. "I'll have to tell Mrs. Larsen sooner or later. Then it will be all over town!"

"Of course, but not through Mrs. Larsen. She hoards; she doesn't give. Also, if you keep her on—you intend to, don't you?"

"Certainly," Cynthia answered, astonished.

"Well, then, as long as she has to keep the job and the wages, it's no big deal. But you have to tell others; your friends can't go on forever wondering where Dad is."

"I hate it—the humiliation, and speculation and people being sorry for you and talking about you over bridge tables, luncheons, dinners. I've seen and heard it all a hundred times."

Viki said, "Nothing lasts long, not even gossip. Three quarters of the people you know have been through the same thing."

"I never thought I'd be one of them." Cynthia flushed with sudden anger. "Between you and your father——" she began.

"Please skip it, Mom," Viki said wearily. Her head ached slightly. "I'll go talk to Jenny. I'll call the office tomorrow. Maybe Dad will be free to see me Wednesday."

She wasn't looking forward to it; at the moment she wasn't looking forward to anything—not even Boston.

Cynthia said, "If you could reason with him . . . he's devoted to you and Jenny."

"As I told Jenny—this isn't my ball game. It's between you and Dad—no matter how wretched we feel about it. And he'll have enough to worry about." She added, "I'm sorry I asked Mac to Peaceable. I'm sorry for all of us—you, him, Gran, Reba——"

"Reba!"

"You thought she wouldn't know? And for Dad."

"I had to tell him," Cynthia said defensively.

"I know, I know. It would have been kinder to him if you hadn't; kinder to Gran too. This is *my* ball game, Mac's and mine. We'll have to come to our own decision, just as you and Dad will have to. Your problem has nothing to do with me or Mac."

"You're so hard," said Cynthia after a moment. "All your generation is hard. You frighten me. When I was your age——"

"No one," said Viki, "is ever anyone else's age, except physically." She got to her feet and said ruefully, "It's all such a mess. I'll go talk to Jenny."

Cynthia said, "I think I'll drive over and see Harriet Meadows."

Mrs. Meadows, divorced, not remarried, was a calm, quiet woman who lived alone in a big house except for daytime servants. She was Cynthia's closest friend, though she was older than Cynthia. Her children had grown and were scattered about: one in England, one in California, the youngest in Connecticut. Harriet rarely came to the Warrens' parties. She said unattached women were a nuisance. Now and then she gave a small party herself, and Cynthia and Edward were always invited. Edward found her pleasant, if uninteresting. Cynthia, when first she knew Harriet, had often asked her advice, occasionally about Viki or Jenny, often about social activities, never about Edward. Nor had Harriet ever explained when or why she had divorced her husband, before Cynthia met her.

Cynthia wasn't going to ask Harriet's advice now; she was simply going to tell her what eventually everyone in the neighborhood, and beyond it, would learn.

"I'll see you when you get back," Viki said. She thought: Maybe Mrs. Meadows can help. She's strong as a rock. She'd said that once to her father and Edward had answered, "Yes, indeed; an admirable woman."

Viki went upstairs and knocked on Jenny's bedroom door and Jenny said, "Who is it? Go away."

"Just me," Viki said, and went in uninvited.

"I don't want to talk," Jenny told her. She still caught her breath in small sobs. She was curled up on her bed with Maisie close beside her. Maisie was her confidante in joy, sorrow, anger, rebellion. Viki sometimes wondered what Jenny would do at Blue Mountain without Maisie.

She sat down on the bed and pushed Jenny's hair back from her forehead. She said, "Jenny, it isn't the end of the world."

169

"Well, it's the end of something." Jenny sat up. Her cheeks and her long lashes were wet. "You might have told me," she complained.

"Mom asked me not to. She wanted to herself," said Viki and crossed her fingers.

"When did this all happen?"

"Thursday night."

"You mean to say Dad came to breakfast Friday as usual and then split."

"That's right."

"Did he tell you?"

"No. But, I overheard things Thursday night, and after breakfast I talked to Mom."

"I thought she acted funny," said Jenny thoughtfully. "Does Gran know? Is that why Mom went barrelling up to Peaceable?"

"Yes, she knows."

"Can't she *do* something?"

Viki said, "Jenny, no one can run interference."

"Everyone will know," said Jenny, hugging her knees still touchingly childish, as was the curve of her cheek. "Florence will say . . . That Florence! Always bragging about how well her parents get on . . . how lucky she is—and me too—to have just one set of them." Jenny sat up straighter. "Has Dad gone and got mixed up with a woman again?" she demanded.

"What makes you ask that?"

"Well, years ago—we still had Bessie—he was away for a while. I don't remember how long. Bessie was very mysterious about it. When I asked, she'd say, 'Ask me no questions and I'll tell you no lies.' I don't remember much, but after all, I was maybe seven. . . ."

Viki said, "Whatever he and Mom want us to know, we'll know, sooner or later."

"How can they do this to us?" wailed Jenny.

Viki thought: Or to themselves? "I don't know. Their life together isn't built around us, Jenny."

"Some parents' lives are," said Jenny stubbornly.

"I suppose so; or it seems so. Jenny, believe me, this will work out." She thought: What an idiotic phrase. When I used it to Mom, she wasn't having any.

"You mean they'll get back together?"

"Perhaps. I don't know." She thought of the T'ang horse and of Humpty Dumpty. But sometimes some things could be mended, painfully, and the lesions didn't even show, at least on the surface.

Jenny said, "I never dreamed this could happen to us. I was as smug as Florence. I wasn't even 'specially sorry for kids whose parents split or who had stepfathers or mothers—some, several. . . . I hadn't given up on the Cape yet. But I will now. It's going to be a horrible summer. I'll hate every minute of it."

"No, you won't. Florence will be back, and Bo, maybe. You'll ride—you can swim at the Club—you'll work—go to parties."

"Maybe I won't feel like it. If only you were going to be here, but you're off to Boston and Mac."

"Yes."

"Mom doesn't like the idea, does she?"

"No."

"Is that why you're going to see Dad?"

"Well, partly."

"We're all screwed up," said Jenny. "Doesn't Mom like Mac? I thought he was madly attractive," Jenny said, "the one time he came here."

"I think so too."

"Mom doesn't?"

"No."

Jenny went suddenly scarlet with excitement. She said, "You're going to marry him. Mom's put the hex on it. You're going to ask Dad!"

"No," said Viki. "You see too many movies."

"I suppose it's all none of my business," Jenny said, deflated.

Viki hugged her. "I'd tell you if I were going to marry Mac with or without parental permission, honey," she said.

"Maybe I'll never get married, but if I do I know exactly what he'll be like," Jenny told her.

"Steve McQueen?"

"Don't be silly. Not too good-looking, and at least five years older. Money too. I want no part of a walk-up pad with cockroach decor. Florence—she'd settle for anyone and right now wouldn't be too soon. You know why she likes to have me around?"

"Can't imagine. Why?"

"Guys," Jenny explained. "What else? I'm a lot prettier than Florence, so you'd think she'd avoid me like poison. Not so. The guys come around and she's part of the scene. Also, she's available."

"Jenny!"

"Well, I don't know that anyone has found it out yet, but the day will come. All she thinks about is sex," Jenny said scornfully. "And of course she's smart. . . . I'm glad she isn't going to Blue Mountain."

"You're a dreadful child," Viki said lovingly. "Mom said you couldn't stand Florence."

"I can't."

"Then why are you practically inseparable?"

"Same reason. Guys. I like to have them around too, but I'm *not* available. I won't be until there's a diamond, also platinum band. I'm smarter than Florence in that respect."

Viki looked at her with considerable admiration. Jenny would probably get what she wanted in her own way.

"I don't want kids," said Jenny. "At least the way I feel now I don't. I might change my mind, but that's light years off. Viki, please tell Dad we love him."

"I shall. Mom's gone out to see Mrs. Meadows. You try and get some sleep."

"At this hour? With all that's happened?"

"Well, play records, look at television, read—I have a headache; I'm going to bed. I'll hear Mom come in."

She thought, going into her own room: Jenny's desolate and stunned. But it's all very dramatic to her. She's like a rubber ball; you depress her, let go, and she bounces back. But she will have a miserable summer, poor kid, unless there's excitement revolving solely around her.

Viki undressed, showered, and lay flat on her bed, listening to her radio. Ray Price, singing "for the good times." She turned off the music and lay there in the dark. She could hear Jenny's stereo. Once, she fell into light uneasy sleep, but woke when she heard her mother's car drive up.

When Cynthia came upstairs, Viki was out in the hall. "You all right, Mom?" she asked.

"Yes." She added, low, "Come with me for a moment, Viki."

In her room, Cynthia said, "Jenny's taking the situation very badly."

"Yes, for now, anyway."

"Your father is unspeakably selfish—and you have been too, Viki."

Viki was silent and then Cynthia said, "I told Harriet —about my situation. She has, I suppose, a remarkably sane viewpoint, not that I can agree with her. There was very little discussion. I just wanted her to know before someone else told her." She did not add that Harriet had said in her unhurried way, coming as close to a confidence as she'd ever had, "Don't try to hold him, Cynthia. . . . If you have to try, it isn't worth it. I learned that a long time ago."

Viki said, "I'm glad you went to see her. Good night, Mom."

"Good night," said her mother and Viki went out and closed the door behind her. Doors were always closing, she thought—or opening.

16

AT TEN ON TUESDAY MORNING, Viki called her father's office and was put through to his secretary, Mrs. Gibson. She'd known Mrs. Gibson for a long time, and having often been in the office, could visualize her sitting in her own little sanctum, guarding the Boss's door, and, at another, less important desk, whatever assistant she happened to have.

"It's Viki, Mrs. Gibson."

"I know. How nice to hear your voice."

"Dad said to call him this morning."

"He's tied up for the moment. I'll get back to you."

Viki replaced the telephone and waited. Jenny came in, and asked, "You call Dad?"

"Yes. He was busy; he'll call me. Do you want to speak to him, Jenny?"

Jenny's eyes brimmed. "No, I don't. Honestly. I just can't."

"All right."

Jenny went out, and Viki heard her running downstairs. She had no idea where Cynthia was. She looked around the study and wondered if she wanted to take anything from it to Boston. No, just her clothes, radio, and things from her dressing table.

When the telephone rang, she jumped and her heart hammered. She said, "Hello?"

"Viki?" asked Mrs. Gibson. "Your father's on the line."

"Thanks. . . . Hello, Dad."

Somehow she'd expected that his voice would have altered, but it was the same voice she had heard for twenty years. "Viki," he asked, "would you come here to the office about noon tomorrow? I've cleared the decks."

Oh, no, you haven't, she thought, except maybe of us. Aloud she said, "That's fine."

"We'll talk here for a while. I'll tell Mrs. Gibson I'm not to be disturbed. Then I'll take you to lunch. Any special place?"

"No, Pop," she said, and that was a special term.

"How about The Two Brothers? You used to like it, and it's still there—quiet, good food and service, I hope. I haven't been for some time, but we'll risk it. Is Jenny there?"

"She just went out. I don't know where."

"Give her my love."

The conversation was concluded. Viki opened the door to the hall, and her mother was outside, patently eavesdropping, and making no attempt at concealment or excuse.

"When are you going to see him, Viki?"

"Tomorrow. I'm to be at the office about noon, then we'll have lunch."

"I suppose the indispensable Mrs. Gibson will arrange everything. I wonder what she thinks."

"Why should she think anything?"

"She knows your father," said Cynthia. "I hope you don't intend to drive in. Parking's impossible, and garages full up by practically dawn."

"I rarely drive in. I'll take the train. There's one which will get me there in plenty of time."

"You'll come right back after lunch?"

Viki hesitated. "I thought I'd go see Pam Jenkins. She's working in Harlem in a neighborhood house. She could give me some pointers."

"Harlem?" repeated Cynthia horrified. "You know it's not safe!"

"Neither is Madison or Fifth or Park, for that matter. I won't stay long. Pam will be busy. I'll call her this evening at her apartment and ask if she can see me."

"Isn't she the colored girl you brought home once?"

"Yes. She's Karen's roommate, and a good friend of mine."

"She seemed very pleasant," said Cynthia. "Well, it stays light for a long time." She hesitated. "But be sure you're not late."

"I won't be. I'll take a train from One hundred and Twenty-fifth Street."

They were courteous, matter-of-fact, and remote. Cynthia turned away. She said, "I thought I'd take you and Jenny to the Club for lunch. You can swim first, if you like."

"That would be nice."

"Jenny needs cheering up, poor child," Cynthia said.

Viki went back to her room to look for a swim suit. She thought: I'll get through today, and even tomorrow, and then Thursday, somehow. I'll call the travel bureau and find out about planes. Fred can take me to the airport. I can pack. I can be with Jenny . . . She thought further: I'll call Mac tonight at his house. . . . No, I won't. . . . I'll see him Friday or he'll call me at Karen's. There's nothing I can say to him over the phone.

The following morning Cynthia had a migraine, and Edna took her a breakfast tray. Jenny was unusually silent at breakfast, and Viki talked a great deal about nothing in particular, when Mrs. Larsen or Edna were in the dining room.

"Like my city getup?"

Dark, plain, thin, with short sleeves and a jacket.

"I'm not used to you looking like The Establishment. You going to wear a hat?"

"That far, I won't go. Gloves, however."

"You'll tell me all about your date when you come home?"

"Of course." Viki crossed her fingers for the second time.

Jenny brightened. She said, "Well, yesterday at the Club wasn't bad. I haven't laid eyes on Dave Graham for months. He's grown a foot. He said he'd been in Maine since college let out."

"How old is he?"

Jenny scowled slightly. "I don't remember. He was a class ahead of me in Country Day. I suppose, nineteen."

"He's quite a charmer."

"That's what he thinks." Jenny paused. "He asked me if I'd like to go dancing at the Club a week from Saturday."

"And?"

"Natch. But of course I said I didn't know; I'd have to look at my engagement book. My theory is, let 'em sweat a little. He'll call me." She added that she was riding with Florence this morning. "But I'll come home for lunch."

"When are they going to the Cape?"

"Don't even speak about it. . . . Friday."

VIKI TOOK THE VW to the railroad station and left it there in a huddle of cars. The train was late, as usual. Walking along the platform, she thought an appointment such as the one she was about to keep must be like surgery—not that she remembered much about her one experience in an operating room, for the removal of tonsils. But certainly you went in with misgivings, wondering if you'd come out alive. Well, it wasn't quite that; of course, the patient was heavily sedated

178

even before she or he reached the table. Viki wasn't sedated; she was nervous and apprehensive and sorry she'd had bacon and eggs for breakfast.

She took a taxi from Grand Central to her father's office. When she opened the door to the reception room, she spoke to the woman at the desk, and to the younger one at the switchboard. She knew them by name and they said how glad they were to see her, and how well she was looking. Mrs. Gibson came out briskly, and Jenny kissed her firm, slightly scented cheek. "It's been years," said Mrs. Gibson.

"Easter holidays."

"Well, it seems years. Come on in; your father's waiting."

The anteroom was just the same, except there was no one at the other desk.

"What happened to Miss Perez?"

"Matrimony. I didn't look for a replacement—I don't really need anyone, and we're cutting down like everyone else."

Edward came from his office, put his arm around Viki's shoulders, and said, "Come on in," and to Mrs. Gibson, "No calls. . . . You booked a table?"

"Yes, Mr. Warren."

He took Viki into the office and shut the door. She walked over to look from the windows. This was a big building, much glass, many floors. The agency office was close to the top. Nothing had changed since Easter. The big desk, the other furniture, the pictures, the conventional family photographs—Cynthia, Viki, Jenny, and an enlarged snapshot of Lucy and Sam taken in Spain, laughing, the sun slanting down, flowers all around them, trees. . . .

"Sit down, honey."

She sat in the chair opposite the polished scrupulously neat desk, and looked at him. He looked the same, perhaps a little tired. She expected she looked the same, but not tired.

"You're looking very well, Viki."

"I am."

"How's Jenny?"

"About as you'd think she'd be, Dad."

He said nothing. "Well, we're both in a hell of a spot—you and I."

"That's right. . . . Aren't you going to ask me anything?"

"Are you happy, Viki?"

"Not at the moment," she answered.

"Nor I. . . . I think I remember young McDonald. . . . He came to the house once at Christmastime, didn't he? . . . I liked him."

"Yes. He liked you too."

"I can't sort out how I feel about him now."

"Sometimes I can't either, if for different reasons."

"It's true, of course, what your mother told me?"

"Yes."

"Do you and Mac have any plans?"

"Marriage, you mean? . . . No. She must have told you that too."

"She did. . . . Why not, Viki?"

"He can't afford it."

"If money's all that prevents you kids from marrying——"

"It isn't. I could manage, though he wouldn't like that. But it's more than money. It's his age and mine. Lots of people we know marry young, and scrape along. I don't want that; he doesn't want it. And I don't want to be married for a long time yet, Dad—to him or anyone else. I want to study, work, play."

"You don't love him?" he asked, incredulous and shocked.

180

"Of course. Gran says I don't; she says I'm just in love and that there's a difference."

"She's right, of course. The difficulty is to get it straight in your mind and emotions."

"Mom," said Viki, expressionless, "says it's sex."

"Well, that too, of course," he agreed unhappily, "but only a part of it, I'm sure, knowing you."

"That's right." She added, "After all that's happened in such a short time, I'm up to here with nagging questions, anger, frustration—all mine. So I don't know how I feel."

"How will you feel when you see him again?"

"Happy," she said simply, "but still mixed up."

"Shall I come to Boston after a while?"

"If you want to, Dad."

"Actually, I don't," he admitted. He didn't want to see Mac; he didn't want to see Mac and Viki together—it would be awkward, embarrassing, and very painful. He thought; Cynthia is better off than I am. No imagination.

"Then don't." She smiled suddenly. "I'll be back home before I return to school. It's—well—just this summer. I haven't the remotest idea what will or won't happen. I just think of it as . . . *the* summer."

"But when you go back to college——"

She said, "Oh, we'll see each other, provided the summer hasn't built barriers: boredom, or mutual—even one-sided—satiety. But the senior year's a sort of madhouse of activities and we both have to study hard, long, and seriously. Even if the summer's all I thought it might be before I went to Peaceable—we won't be able to be together as much as we have been."

He said, "Whatever happens or doesn't happen, you can count on me, Viki."

"Yes, I know." She looked at him soberly. "I didn't think it would be like this."

"Like what?"

"Us, talking. Oh, I knew you wouldn't beat me or throw me out of the window, but I thought——"

"Recriminations? How could you do such a terrible thing, and all that?"

"I suppose so."

"You don't know me very well, after all," he said. "I haven't been Sir Galahad, myself . . . as you know now."

"I knew nine years ago."

He was silent for a moment. Then said, "I'm sorry, Viki."

"It's all right." She asked, with an effort, "What's going to happen to you and—and her?"

"Her name's Lisa," he said. "She's thirty-two and works on a fashion magazine. She was married for a short time when she was eighteen. She wants—God help her—to marry me."

Viki thought about that; she didn't like thinking about it, but she did and then asked, "Do you want to marry her?"

"Sometimes yes, and sometimes no," he said wearily. "On the tough, practical side, I don't suppose I could afford it, even if your mother would consent to a divorce."

She said, "Everything's up in the air, isn't it?"

"It is. Your mother's told Jenny?"

"Yes . . . She—Mom, I mean—wants you to come see Jenny."

"I shall, of course, or ask her to come here. Is she unhappy?"

"She's miserable, Pop . . . but she'll get over it, or, most of it——"

He rose and went to the windows, and she turned to watch him, but remained where she was. He said, over his shoulder, "We haven't gotten very far, have we?"

"No."

"Suppose we leave it as it is, for the summer? It won't cause a nine days' wonder. A great many people separate; sometimes they decide to get back together again; other times, to stay apart, divorce, or just separate legally. Perhaps by this fall, I'll have made up my mind, or your mother may have changed hers—who knows? And you will find out if one summer really lasts forever."

Viki rose, crossed the room, and put her arms around him, and held him not hard, but reassuringly and gently, as if she were the parent. Here eyes were dry. His were not.

Presently she went into the private bathroom, washed her face, brushed her hair, reddened her mouth, and they went out through the anteroom. "If there's anything really important," Ed Warren told Mrs. Gibson, "you know where to reach me."

Viki said good-bye, and Mrs. Gibson admonished, "Don't stay away so long this time."

Viki and her father went down in the elevator and took a taxi to the restaurant.

There they talked a great deal about nothing, and had lunch. As they were finishing, he asked, "Are you going right home?"

"No." She told him where she planned to go, and he said, "I remember that black girl as very beautiful."

"Yes, and immensely popular. Everyone likes her."

He looked up to find their waiter and order coffee. That was when he saw Lisa. She was leaving, alone, the smaller of the two dining rooms.

Coincidence? Not by a damn sight. He'd never been here with Lisa, nor had he ever heard her mention the place. She preferred livelier, more "in" bistros. There was no explanation other than that she or her secretary had called the office after he'd left, talked to Mrs. Gibson, and been told

183

where Mr. Warren would be if it was urgent to reach him. In which case, Lisa's timing was little short of miraculous. He and Viki had probably been in the elevator. A surge of anger seized him, hard as a sudden blow, hot as the coffee their waiter had just poured.

Viki saw his face alter, his mouth tighten. She asked, "Is anything the matter, Dad?"

"No. I was just thinking that my next client is going to be difficult, if not impossible. . . . Well, we'll have our coffee. Then I'll take care of the check and find you a taxi. I'll walk back to the office. I have time, and I can work off my annoyance and greet the client with 'becks and nods and wreathed smiles.' I hope that's how it goes. In other words, I'll cool it."

He lingered over the coffee, letting it cool. The check came, and he fished out his credit card. . . . Wait a little. Not that Lisa would be lurking in the small lobby, to discover him with startled pleasure and remark, "What a surprise running into you here, Mr. Warren!" and then look with bright inquiry at Viki, pending an introduction.

No. Lisa was too clever for that, but she hadn't been clever enough.

He took Viki to the street and the doorman whistled up a cab. When it came, her father kissed her and put her into it. He said, "Keep in touch. Be sure to send me the Boston address and telephone number. Give Jenny my love—and take a lot of it to Boston with you. And tell Jenny we'll have a date soon. I'll call her."

"Thanks, Pop," Viki said, "thanks for everything."

17

VIKI GAVE THE DRIVER the address and resigned herself to a long, hot, noisy, probably hair-raising trip uptown. The car was one in which the driver was protected from the potentially dangerous passenger, but this driver apparently decided Viki was no menace. He looked at her appreciatively and wondered who the man was. Father? Relative? Family friend? He hoped not boy friend, but one never knew. He managed in spite of the glass partition between them to talk to her about everything. New York was for the birds. Did she live here? He discoursed on the deplorable state of the taxi industry, the perils, the lack of reward, and dwelt for a time on the long hours, the rides to hell-and-gone, airports, Brooklyn, Queens . . . and spoke sadly of the shrinkage in tips.

Viki answered as best she could. Most of the time she couldn't hear him; but she nodded or shook her head, smiled, and looked sympathetic. And when she reached her destination, he said, "Better be careful, Miss; this ain't the greatest neighborhood in town—but then which is?"

Viki thanked and overtipped him. He drove away happy, wondering about her, and whistling in retrospect.

She'd believed she could think in the cab despite traffic, bone-jarring stops, horns, and altercations between drivers. But it had been impossible. She'd think on the train, she told herself, or driving home.

Pam, in the neighborhood house, could give her some time, so they sat in Pam's little office and talked about their friends and what everyone was doing, and how it would be as seniors.

"Have you seen Mac, Viki?"

"Briefly. He came to my grandmother's when I was there last weekend."

"What's he doing?"

Viki told her, and Pam said, "Sounds great. You'll see him this summer?"

"Oh, yes. I'm going to Boston to work, Friday."

"Very likable guy," Pam remarked. "What kind of work?"

Viki told her, and added frankly, "I'm scared I'll be an outsider. I wonder if I can handle the job? How about a little briefing? You've been working here since your freshman year, vacations, summers; you're a pro, and I need guidance."

"I'm flattered, Viki, but you don't, really. You already have what it takes."

"Such as what?"

"For one thing," Pam said, laughing, "you're quite beautiful, which helps."

"We are not amused," Viki told her regally. "But speaking of that, so are you. I had lunch with my father today. He said just that; he remembers you vividly."

Pam smiled. She was an exceptionally attractive young woman. "That just about makes my day—that, and seeing you," she said.

"I'm waiting for you to tell me my other qualifications."

"You like people; that's very important. You're not sentimental. You're a good listener—I often think of our rap sessions. You get along with almost everyone, I think. So that's what you'll be doing. Getting along with—and learning from —people who need advice, who want to talk. Kids who are looking for help, for a little fun, and brief escape from their environments and family problems. I've discovered no matter how much they yell and holler about it, they actually want some sort of reasonable discipline. It makes them feel someone cares about them, and that's real security. You'll get on with your boss or bosses too, if you just remember they are also human and vulnerable. They get tired, irritated, and discouraged, and none is God or even Solomon. Honestly, you'll love the work."

"I hope so, and I'll try to give satisfaction," Viki said, smiling.

"Good. Give my love to Karen. I could murder her. Tell her she might manage five minutes now and then to write me. I love that girl, but when we're not in school, she seems to vanish into thin air."

"I'll write, Pam. I have your home address."

"It's a hot noisy walk-up. I share it with a couple of other girls. But it's heaven once I get back there, kick my shoes off, and turn on the radio. . . . Viki, take care."

That was good-bye for the summer.

Viki went out, smiling, and a tall black boy appeared as if by magic and said, "Miss Jenkins wants I should get you a taxi."

"Well, thanks," said Viki. "What's your name?"

"Sam."

Sam whistled shrilly and kept it up until a cab came along. Viki opened her handbag and then thought better of it. Sam was proudly fulfilling a request; he had a mission.

She shook his thin hand and said, "Thanks, Sam.

I probably would have waited hours if it hadn't been for you. Thank Miss Jenkins for me too."

He answered with a wide grin, "Sure will, Man, she's the Most."

When Viki's train came, she got into a smoker, the nearest car. It wasn't, of course, clean, nor was it air-conditioned. People trooped in and sat down and she looked at long hair, short hair, Civil War beards, Apostle beards, and every kind of costume, from the usual blue jeans, purposely ragged shorts, Indian headbands, long printed skirts, shifts. . . . It was close, smoky, and vocal. Thank heaven her ride would be brief.

She found herself interested in the couple opposite her. The girl, nondescript and eating a strawberry ice-cream cone, wore long hair, sandals, and a short shift; her barefoot escort's hair was longer than hers, his facial decoration was a small thick mustache. He wore faded patched shorts pulled out at the hems. Very chic. Also a T-shirt which matched his girl's ice cream, and which was printed in black with some sort of emblem—Viki couldn't identify it—also in black. But the printed message in dubious French was loud and clear, "Faites l'amour pas la guerre."

Viki smiled. This was the first time she'd seen the words in a language other than her own.

Reaching her station, she stepped from the overcrowded car to the platform and the VW was waiting for her, a look of reproach on its blunt front and rear. She said, "Sorry about that. Well, out, out, and away!"

The massed cars were still there, awaiting, to paraphrase Mr. Field, the touch of an owner's hand. Sometimes hands, not the owner's, managed a little stealing or stripping, even here.

When she reached home, Fred was there. He took the car and she went in, determined to shed her city clothes as soon as possible. She hadn't done any thinking in the train. Who could?

Jenny was in their study and popped out. "How was the trip?" she inquired.

"Hot, noisy. Fortunately the train wasn't filled with commuters—it was a little early for that—just old gals with shopping bags, frustrated salesmen and a lot of kids en route to a rock-do or a happening, or just en route."

"Don't stall." Jenny dragged her into the study and shut the door. "What did Dad say? Is he coming home?"

"I don't know whether he is or not, Jenny." Watching her sister's young eager face fall, she added, "Give him time, dear."

"Parents!" said Jenny vigorously. "I suppose we have to have them, but how selfish can you be? I'm sick of crying and wondering and thinking about my friends and everything. It's rotten!"

"Hold it. Dad's coming out to see you or he'll make a date with you to see him in town. He'll call you. He sent his love."

"Great," Jenny remarked bitterly. "Just erase the works, 'specially your family. Nice knowing you. Don't call me, I'll call you. . . . I thought you could persuade him."

"I didn't even try. Now, I've got to get out of this dress."

"I simply don't understand you!" Jenny said.

"Where's Mom?"

"Still in her room, I guess. She's harder hit than we are. But then I don't understand her either—or him."

Cynthia, her migraine somewhat abated, came down for dinner. She looked ill and drawn, and ate only what she had ordered for herself: clear broth, hot tea, dry toast. When Mrs. Larsen and Edna were absent, she asked Viki politely, "How was your trip?"

"Miserable. But" she added hastily, "I survived. I mean, it was hot and noisy, the traffic terrible as you'd expect, and the train jammed, coming back."

"How is your father?"

"All right; just a little tired, I think." She remarked that the office was cool, "but I really don't like air-conditioning. I should have taken a sweater; my little jacket's worthless. It was like Alaska in winter at the restaurant."

"Where did you go?" Jenny asked.

"The Two Brothers. You remember it. Dad took us all there one spring vacation."

"Dreamy," Jenny recalled, "divine food."

Cynthia remembered The Two Brothers. She'd been there with Edward. Portrait of a well-turned-out suburban housewife meeting her successful husband for dinner, the theater, a night on the town. Sometimes they'd stayed in overnight.

Cynthia finished her tea and decided to go back to bed. "Come up when you've finished, Viki. I want to talk to you."

After she had left the room, Jenny predicted, not without a certain satisfaction, "Now, you're in for it."

"Could be. I hope not. Poor thing, she looks wretched."

When later Viki knocked at Cynthia's door and was told to enter, she found her in bed, an ice bag riding rather rakishly on the red head.

"Wouldn't you rather talk tomorrow? Perhaps you'll feel better then."

"Oh, I shall. This misery never lasts more than three days. But I want to talk now. What happened?"

Viki, on the end of the chaise, answered, "Nothing, really."

"I'm not asking about you. I'm sure your father said he

was distressed and hurt, but that he understood. Funny," she added reflectively, "he's like your grandmother sometimes and he's only her son-in-law. Perhaps that's why they get on so well. Actually, I don't suppose he could do anything else —he's hardly in a position to moralize. Did you ask him if he still insists on marrying that tramp, knowing I won't consent to a divorce?"

Viki answered equably, "I did ask if he wanted to marry her, Mom. He said, in effect, he didn't know."

Cynthia moved her head abruptly against the pillows and the ice bag slid to the floor. Viki rose to retrieve it. It was getting dark now, and Cynthia switched on the small pink night-light at the base of the bedside lamp. "Never mind," she said, "let it go. . . . Well, if he isn't sure, I can wait until he is, one way or another."

"Suppose it's the other way, not yours?"

"I'll cross that bridge when I come to it," she answered, and Viki thought: It will be a large bridge, over a big chasm.

"Meantime," Cynthia went on, "I'll stay right here, except for taking Jenny to Peaceable or someplace, for a weekend." She didn't want to go to her mother's; perhaps Jenny would settle for a weekend on the Cape? "I'll go on with my life," she added, "such as it is. Our friends, our acquaintances, the help, even the tradespeople will learn, eventually that your father and I have separated. I'll tell a few; it will be repeated . . . news gets around. That's all they need know," she said firmly.

Chalk one up for her, Viki thought. Her mother was running true to form. She wouldn't rush around confiding in all and sundry, explaining, martyred, that Edward had left her for another woman. She had too much pride. Keep on smiling. Wait. It will all come right, for right's on my side.

It was a pretty fair evaluation, but what Viki didn't

know was that Cynthia was like her paternal grandmother, and also the product of her own parents. There was loyalty, beyond pride; in her case, loyalty to a code.

She won't give herself away, Viki thought.

Cynthia asked, "Did he say he'd come to see Jenny?"

"Yes—or have her to lunch in town. He'll telephone."

"Did he—seem"—she hesitated over the next word, selected a tepid one—"sorry?"

"I think so, yes, for us all."

"I don't mean that. Perhaps I mean guilty."

"I don't know, Mom," said Viki wearily.

Cynthia dismissed her and Viki went to her room. Jenny popped in to ask, "Fireworks? Atomic bomb?"

"No, Idiot. I'm pooped. Take yourself to bed, or if not, keep the radio low and, for heaven's sake, no hard rock on the stereo."

"To listen is to obey. You're getting old, Big Sister."

Alone in her room, Viki thought: So I am, and wished that she were not a disillusioned twenty, but eight years old. No tragedies, no situations, no dramas, except those she created for herself in daydreams. She wished she were a child, mindless, running through the field or orchards at Peaceable, singing to herself, and feeling the sense of unreasoning joy which she had not known since, except in rare, momentary flashes.

Before she slept she thought of her father. It had been rough for him today. At luncheon, during their desultory impersonal conversation, he'd said he had a client coming to the Club for dinner that night. "He's old, he's persnickety, he can't stand the usual restaurants. So I'll soothe him with masculine trappings . . . not that the Club didn't yield some years ago, and admit women for lunch and dinner. But there's still a small dining room sacred to the male."

She thought: I don't suppose he was telling the truth.

192

❦ 18

EDWARD HAD TOLD THE TRUTH. He had a long, dull, but ultimately rewarding dinner in the air-conditioned, exclusively male dining room of his Club. They had cold soup, cold roast beef, a salad, a hot vegetable, cheese, crackers, and coffee. They drank a pitcher of Sangria. His client didn't care for the hard stuff.

Lisa was speaking at a small, elegant dinner of fashion editors. He was to meet her later at her apartment.

He went there, after the client had departed in an old, beautiful Rolls, and after fortifying himself with a cognac at the bar. He hoped Lisa would have reached home—"I won't be late, darling; we're all working people"—as she had not permitted him a key to the apartment. She had said, "No, that wouldn't do, however convenient." After all, if people saw him using a key. . . . She didn't know her next-door neighbor except to speak to; but neighbors had friends, relatives, guests, and any one of these might know Edward.

He thought, walking uptown in the warm moonlight, that it would be awkward to hang around the lobby, or even to have to go away and return. Callers were announced in this type of building.

He walked slowly, keeping an eye on doorways, an ear on following footsteps, even in this neighborhood. He thought of Viki and his heart stung. Poor kid—foolish, happy, unhappy! Everything had come at the wrong time. Viki's situation —he thought of it as Cynthia's fault; why had Cynthia had to discover it?—his own defection. . . . I suppose that's what you'd call it, he thought.

He'd dreaded seeing his wife Sunday night, dreaded seeing Viki today, but he didn't dread seeing Lisa, because if you're angry, you're not afraid.

When he reached the building she had, the doorman told him, just come in, so he went up in the elevator, exchanging pleasantries with the operator, and pressed the chimes button. There were only two apartments on this floor.

Lisa opened the door saying, "Ten minutes earlier and you would have had to wait. Come in and be comfortable. I have to refresh my face. I've spent all evening looking interested, excited, showing all my front teeth. A couple of my dearest enemies were there, very competent fencers. My so-called speech was short and to the point, if any."

As she blew him a kiss, he sat down and looked around the room. A few of the things in it he'd given her: a small bright painting not particularly valuable, which they'd seen in a little gallery and she had coveted for its color and size—"I've just the wall space for it"; a silver cigarette box unmarked—it would not have been discreet to order names or dates; a crystal bowl, which he'd sent her full of roses. He noticed idly that some of the Club matches were in the mauve ashtray with the matching cigarette container which he'd given her very recently, on the Bucks County weekend.

Lisa came out of her room; he rose and she waited for him to take her in his arms. He did not. She smiled, sat down, and said, "You've had a miserable day, darling."

"What makes you think so?"

"Oh, you're wearing your grim look and you aren't interested in me at the moment. . . . How was Viki?"

"She's very well as you must have noticed when you saw her."

"When I saw her——" she began. It was a mistake, and she knew it. She shrugged. "You're angry," she said.

"Very. I saw you leaving the other dining room——"

"I thought I was being so careful!"

"Not careful enough. You should have left after we did. Apparently you could see us from where you were sitting."

"Yes, but I had to leave. I had an appointment. . . . I can't see why you're so upset."

"You aren't stupid, as a rule."

Her color rose and her voice. "I wanted to get a look at her," she said. "What's so indecent about that? So I had Lynn call your office and say it was important—having to do with layouts. Mrs. Gibson told her where you'd be."

"I figured that out."

"For heaven's sake, sit down. Don't stand there looming over me. I just wanted to see her, that's all. She looks like you, darling."

He said, "I'm astonished that you didn't wait in ambush to greet me with amazement, thereby insuring an introduction!"

"Stupid I may be, as you've just remarked, but not that stupid."

He sat down rather heavily, and Lisa curled her feet under her and locked her hands around her knees. "I still don't understand why you're making a scene."

"I'm not. But a scene in the restaurant would have been a bad one. Viki knows about you—she would certainly have guessed who you are. Jenny knows, too, and in a very short time I imagine a great many others will also. Not about you personally—Cynthia doesn't confide in people—but the simple fact of our separation."

She said carelessly, "Well, it had to come out sooner or later. I'm sorry about your girls, but it was only natural that their mother would tell them."

"I don't like being spied on, Lisa, not by anyone."

"I wasn't spying." She put her hands over her face and began to cry. She did not plan it; it was not a strategy; it was merely because she'd had a rotten evening and there was one woman she hadn't outfenced. She'd not been happy, peering through masses of foliage at Edward and his tall, quite lovely daughter. She had looked forward to coming back here and being comforted for everything she'd never had, or had lost, and afterwards to being stimulated into excitement and pleasure.

Edward Warren was tired of women who wept. He was tired of women, period. But he rose, went over, picked her up, and sat down again, holding her.

"All right," he said. "We won't talk about it any more."

"I'm sorry," she said. "I'm truly sorry."

She was. It had been a blunder, but she was sorry mainly for herself.

Women in her position couldn't afford blunders. You'd think they could, you'd think they had the whip hand. They didn't. She'd learned that the hard way.

She didn't want this to end. She couldn't bear it. She wanted Edward Warren, and also what he stood for, which was security—not just money, he'd been plain-spoken about that. As of now her position on the magazine seemed safe enough, but one never knew. The uncertainty of jobs had been discussed at the dinner that night, among themselves—here today, gone tomorrow. She was, in her field, highly paid. She could go elsewhere—a couple of years ago she would have said, "Of course"—but that wasn't certain now. If she had to find another position—well, there weren't many, and if one were available, she'd have to take a big cut and settle for a lower rung on the ladder. Besides, she was tired of the cat-eat-cat life, which had appealed so much to her at one time. People saying "But how young she is for the job!" She was tired of doing battle with manicured claws, masked for the most part, but not always; of gossip, and rumor; of the mounting costs of her and everyone else's business. She was sick to death of being charming, looking charming, and of knowing the right people. She'd obtained her position by these not unusual tactics, and had loved it. But not now when she had to hang on to it in the same way, never relaxing. She was an enthusiastic exponent of the current female emancipation both in and out of her magazine, but for some time she'd thought a woman better off if she were charming to and for a particular man, if she managed not an office but his household and children, and became so indispensable that her job was for life. This attitude was considered Dark Ages now, but in the long run it paid off. And one would still use strategy tactics, if for different purposes.

Her heart tightened. It hadn't paid off—that is, she hoped it wouldn't—for Cynthia Warren. But she wasn't Cynthia.

She said, "Edward, please forgive me."

She rarely called him by name when they were alone; she used endearments. Now he stroked her hair from her nice forehead, offered her his handkerchief, and said, "It's all right, Lisa."

It wasn't all right, not then or afterward when he lay beside her in the darkness and thought: This isn't enough. But what is?

As he was leaving, she asked drowsily, "When will I see you?"

"I'll have to phone you," he told her. "I may go away for a few days."

She sat bolt upright then. The bedside lamp was on and she looked at him with anxiety, and asked sharply, "You're planning to go home?"

"No."

He wasn't. He'd just decided that he must get away by himself. There was in the Adirondacks a small association to which he belonged, for its fishing and hunting. It had been designed as an escape hatch: no families, no women; just plain, rough living, and not many members. He could fly up, he thought. Then, taking a cab back to the Club, thought further: Tomorrow's Thursday. I'll call the Camp in the morning and see if I can get a cabin for the weekend, starting Friday.

The Adirondacks camp was equipped with one telephone only, in the main structure, which had a simple lounge, a room for fishing gear, and a dining room—one long table and an aperture into the kitchen, where you stood waiting for your plate to be handed to you. The guides cooked.

Breakfast was early; at midday the club members were usually out, armed with sandwiches, beer, and frying pans, in case luck was with them. On rainy days they also went out. But if there was a hard storm when nothing would rise to the flies, they had a radio in the lounge, and card tables were set up. They kept the bar stocked, each member contributing. The club had an Indian name; as long as your arm and it meant, "He who is free on the path."

Mrs. Gibson phoned and talked to the caretaker-manager. Yes, there were cabins, only a few members had made reservations.

She so reported and Edward said, "Good. . . . Look at the timetable, will you, and get me a flight? Cancel my Friday afternoon appointments. . . . How about Monday?"

She told him what his appointments were, and he said, "Cancel. See if they can be postponed; none is important. I'll get back Monday night, or if not, I'll let you know."

"You do look tired," she commented. She added, "Did the *Beau Monde* people reach you? Miss Lewis' secretary called about some layouts."

"Oh, yes," said Edward. "She reached me." And how! he thought. Not the eager, eye-on-the-next-job Lynn, but Miss Lewis herself. He did not want to lose her; he did not want to keep her. The polygamous tribes, races, religions, had something going for them, he thought.

He did not expect an, as yet, unpolluted lake, silence, deep scented woods, brilliant or cloudy skies, quiet and lonely casting and concentration to provide answers to any of his problems. Nor did a change of environment as a rule. But perhaps he could think, consider, weigh, and get everything together. Perhaps not.

That Thursday morning it rained again, a steady straight-falling beneficial rain. Viki packed, and Jenny, disregarding the rain, went off on her bike to say farewell to Florence. "Back for lunch," she said.

Cynthia made a dinner reservation for herself and her daughters at the Inn some miles out of the town. There would be fewer people there whom she knew. The Country Club was always crowded on Thursday nights.

Mrs. Larsen asked if it would be all right if she didn't leave after lunch, except to do some personal shopping. She'd take a taxi, and could she have her nephew for supper in the kitchen?

Cynthia said, of course, and thought with resignation of her taxi bill. Mrs. Larsen didn't own a car. Local taxis took her, on her days off, to the local railroad station, or a bus stop, or shopping.

Mrs. Larsen departed to call Rusty at his mother's. If he were out, he could call back. Her sister had written her that Rusty, poor boy, couldn't find a regular job.

Mrs. Larsen and her sister had one thing in common; a blind spot named Roger, called Rusty. His mother did day work; they had a small half house which Mrs. Larsen had helped her sister buy. Rusty's father had gone over the hill a good many years ago.

In the evening Cynthia drove with the girls to the Inn, a big, tree-guarded old house with an antique shop, a waterfall, and gardens. The food was somewhat better than at the County Club, but Thursday was buffet night, which Cynthia had never liked.

Conversation at the table was not effortless except on Jenny's part. She had an appointment at the hospital with Mrs. Parsons on the following day. "All those interns," she sighed to Viki.

"Some don't speak English."

"Who needs it?" Jenny inquired.

In the powder room before they left Cynthia encountered an acquaintance, who asked, "Where's Edward, dear man? Off somewhere on business?"

Cynthia braced herself. "We've separated, Marty—a sort of trial run."

That would be on page one in Marty's book. She made round eyes and said, "How too awful! I'm so sorry."

"It was by mutual consent," Cynthia explained, smiling. She shrugged and added a trifle maliciously, as she knew a good deal about Marty, "You know how it is at our age; things, including marriage, get a little—well—stale."

Marty, rallying, asked, "Has he moved away?"

"With his business obligations? Of course not. He's in New York, living at his Club. He'll be out to see us often."

This time, if only mentally, it was Cynthia who crossed her fingers.

On the way home, she reported casually, "I ran into Marty Southwick in the powder room. She asked about your father. I told her."

Viki was silent. Jenny shrieked, "Told her what, for Pete's sake? It will be all over the county."

"I told her the truth, simply that we're separated for the time being; after all, it has to be all over the county, as you put it, sooner or later."

Later that evening Mac telephoned Viki. He asked, "Is it all right to talk?"

"Of course."

"I had your letter, but I didn't answer it to Karen's. We can discuss everything when I see you. . . . Sure you don't want me to meet you? Even if you come in early I might get off, but I don't promise."

"No. I'd like to get settled. Would you call Karen for me? You have her number, and it isn't too late. If she's not in, try her early tomorrow. Just remind her that she said she'd leave a key with the super."

Mrs. Larsen's Rusty was given a gourmet meal in the kitchen, after he roared up in his motorcycle. Edna thought he was cute; she had never seen him before. But when supper was over Edna, in response to a look from her superior, was forced to scuttle off to her room. Then Mrs. Larsen said, "Well, I suppose it's money again, Rusty."

It was. He couldn't scrape up the payment due on the color TV. "I gave it to Ma for her birthday," he reminded his aunt. "Now she wants a new fridge." He did not add that the O.T.B. hadn't restored or made his fortune. Besides, it was more fun at the track. He added, by way of apology, that steady work had gone down the drain, and there was his draft status. "Very uncertain," he added sadly.

Mrs. Larsen obliged—for the time being—with sufficient funds to keep the TV running.

FRIDAY WAS CLEAR AND WARM. Edward took to the woods shortly after lunch. Cynthia went to the beauty salon at about the same time, having left Jenny off at the hospital. She'd pick her up later. "If you're through before I get here, just wait."

Jenny would. Waiting in a hospital lobby was sure to be exciting. She didn't give another thought to the Cape. She felt gloriously superior to Florence who wasn't planning to do anything useful this summer, and who in September, would go to an undistinguished college. Smarter than me, thought Jenny, but not where grades are concerned. She couldn't get into Blue Mountain if she tried. I guess she did try. Besides, personality like a hot wet dishcloth.

Friday, an important day, the end of the week, the start of a weekend. Pay day . . . and the commuters' delight. Friday, dedicated to Freya, fairest of the goddesses, goddess of love and youth, also of the dead.

Fred had gone with Viki to the airport before Cynthia and Jenny took off for their appointments. Good-byes were brief; Viki was only going to Boston, not Transylvania.

"Write," said Jenny. "Will you come home weekends?"

" 'Fraid not."

"Telephone me this evening," Cynthia suggested, as she offered a smooth cheek. She could hardly do less with Jenny as a witness.

In the beauty salon, Cynthia saw a few women she knew slightly. They wore pastel smocks, having removed their dresses—if they wore dresses. They sat under dryers, read, wrote letters, confided in manicurists, or directed their hair dressers, male or female, and gossiped too much.

Cynthia asked for fashion magazines and was given several. She did not look at the fashions; she looked at each mast head. All she had to go on was a given name. She found it finally, in *Beau Monde,* and regarded it for a long time: Lisa Lewis . . .

Viki drove the VW to the airport, with Fred beside her. "Take good care of her, Fred. I'm going to miss her. Don't let Jenny practice on her."

He said, "Okay. Trust us."

Once on the plane, Viki felt heavy, smothered, and impatient, as if she herself were an aircraft, solidly socked in, and waiting on the ground. But, after take-off, her heart lifted, her spirit lightened and gained altitude. This was her personal summer, no matter how it progressed or ended.

She looked ahead at blue sky. She soared. She thought: I'll write Jenny. Mom too, but particularly Pop.

She must tell Mac she'd seen her father and that he didn't want to come to Boston. She wouldn't tell him about the family situation, at least not at first; she'd probably have to before September.

Anything could happen before September.

The plane was steady on its course, the earth was left below. A short flight, in sidereal time and air miles, the flight to Boston.

19

Lucy's appointment with her doctor was after lunch. Reba asked, "Sure you don't want me to come with you?"

"Quite sure. What for? To sit in that waiting room and wonder what's the matter with everyone? You'll know most of them."

"You'll tell me what he says, every word?"

"Don't I always?"

Reba watched her drive off. She thought: I don't like it; I don't like it at all. She thought: Don't let anything happen to her, Sam . . . me, first, please. But that wouldn't do. If Lucy were to be left alone, what would happen to her?

Lucy parked at the Library for which Sam had raised the considerable funds. There was an unspoken rule; Mrs. Pemberton could park as long as she wished, ignoring signs, and no questions asked.

From there, she walked to Doctor Harmon's office which was part of his house. She was nervous, and told herself: "Simmer down, or up goes the blood pressure."

Pete would tell her the truth. She'd known him practically forever.

His wife had died twenty years ago. He had a daughter to look after, somewhat older than Cynthia. She was a pediatrician, practicing and living in Vermont with her husband and two children.

Less than two years after Sam's death Pete had asked Lucy if she'd consider marrying him. "We're old friends," he said, "we'd be comfortable together. I suppose I fell in love with you, in a way, the first time I came into your house or maybe when your mother brought you to me before you married Sam."

She was touched, she told him, and very fond of him, but "No, Pete. I'm sorry. I can't."

Six months later he married a widow younger than himself, with whom he'd been seen for a year or two. Nice woman. Good wife. Active, interested, helpful. She'd been a trained nurse and her first husband had also been a doctor in a neighboring town.

Lucy thought: I must remember to ask Pete and Winnie to dinner.

"What are you scared of?" she asked herself. "Cancer?" Well, naturally. Who isn't? Pete's first wife had died of cancer.

"Pain?" Of course. She had a rather low threshold and she couldn't bear anyone else's suffering either, especially Sam's.

"Surgery?" An indignity, an invasion of privacy, a humiliation. Thank God Sam didn't have to go through that; heart surgery hadn't been indicated.

She thought of Cynthia, and of Viki; their problems were her own, only because she loved them. Well . . . she loved Viki, and she was, she supposed, fond of Cynthia. But she couldn't solve things for them.

What will Reba do if I die?

Get along, she decided, walking slowly, seeing the

June brightness, feeling the warmth, regarding the heavy foliage of the trees, not yet dusty, thinking: Suppose I never see June again?

I'm afraid of dying, she admitted, but not of death.

The man ahead of her was hurrying, limping slightly. She had good vision. She wore glasses only for reading, but could even read to some extent without them. She could see the set of the man's shoulder, the way he walked, and also the gesture when he raised a hand in casual greeting to some-one across the street—so like Sam.

In the last ten years there'd always been a stranger walking along a busy street, seen briefly from the window of a bus or a taxi, ahead of her in a crowded airport, or passing by in a car . . . a stranger who seemed to be like Sam. She'd never caught up with him—anywhere.

Now she was hurrying also, quite unconsciously, but the man had turned the corner; he had vanished.

Lucy went on, her pace more temperate. She thought: Well I'll catch up with him someday, and when I do, he will really be Sam.

Her pulse steadied and her breath. She experienced a small, hostile pain, for a moment. She spoke to it in her mind, crossly: "Oh, go 'way," she said.

"You're human," she admonished herself, "so there's always fear and there's always hope." Whatever happens, she thought, I'll accept it, even the bad part, if that's in the cards. I'll make Reba and others miserable. I was never one to suffer in silence. If there's no bad part yet, there are still things I can do: travel, see people, cut flowers, upset poor Reba . . . perhaps, in some way, even help Viki and Cynthia.

She turned another corner and was within two doors of the Harmon house. One red brick path led to Pete's home, the other to his office. She rang the office bell, and went in, as the sign directed. There was no one in the waiting room but Winnie, Pete's wife. On the nurse-secretary's day off she presided, met and talked with patients, answered the telephone, made appointments.

"Hi," said Lucy. "What's wrong? Pete lost his practice?"

"Not yet. He's running late today. We just cleared everyone out. He had a snack at his desk. There was an emergency this morning. You're looking fine, Lucy."

"So why am I here? It's Pete's fault. He said—when was it?—ten days ago that I was to come back for tests. You'd think I was an astronaut or something. Long as I've known your husband he's always been the Norman Rockwell family-doctor type. Better-looking, of course. And he has all the modern conveniences. . . . What do you hear from Evelyn? How are her kids? She's quite a girl."

Winnie agreed, and they spoke of Pete's daughter for a moment. Then Lucy said, "I'll call you tomorrow and pin you down for a date. It's Reba's and my turn to have you for dinner. Pete has to eat sometime, and we won't care how late he is or even if he's called out. We can stay where we are and gossip."

The telephone rang and Lucy retreated to a chair, and looked at a magazine, relieved that there were no other patients who'd be looking uneasy, chatting or silent, some of whom she was bound to know. But after a while the bell rang and two elderly women came in together. Lucy knew them and spoke, thinking: Dear heaven preserve me from getting involved in a discussion of Nell Dylan's ulcers and her sister's nerves.

Miss Dylan had just launched into symptoms when the office door opened and Peter Harmon, tall, somewhat stooped, his white hair thinning, beckoned to Lucy and said, "You're next."

She went into Pete's office and sat down in the chair

facing his. He looked at her and asked, "Why are you so apprehensive?"

"Why not?" she inquired with spirit. "I came to you for an overhaul, and the next thing I know I'm back . . . for tests, you said."

Doctor Harmon shook his head. He said patiently, "Your checkup was fine . . . cardiogram, blood work, chest X ray, the works. You sat right there while I looked at the plate and read the EKG."

Lucy said, "All I complained about was a little pain now and then, and you gave me some tablets."

"That's one reason why you're here. Did they work?"

"Yes, but——"

"Okay. I suspect you're pre-ulcer, Lucy, which is to say you don't have an ulcer yet, but you could have. You can, if you co-operate, eliminate the possibility. . . . I want you to go into the hospital for a few days, to confirm my diagnosis, that's all."

She said indignantly, "Why the hospital? You didn't say a word about this last time."

"I had to get you a room, and I didn't want you to fret about it for a week."

"Ulcers?" she said. "I thought only overworked businessmen, nervous housewives, heavy drinkers and smokers and worriers had them."

Peter laughed. He said, "Your consumption of alcohol is minimal and you don't smoke. But you do worry."

"Hardly ever."

"Nonsense. I've rarely met a non-worrier in my practice or social life."

"Reba will have a fit!"

"Of course, but I'll explain to Reba. Just the tests, Lucy, and then diet, rest, and as little anxiety as is humanly possible. I've already made the preliminary arrangements.

Winnie will call you later today. Suppose we say Monday?"

He rose and Lucy got to her feet. "It's all so unnecessary."

"Not in my book. I'm ninety-nine percent sure, but that isn't enough." He put his arm around her shoulder. "You're a healthy woman, my dear. You'll probably live for ten or fifteen years. All you have to do is take care." He bent his white head, kissed her cheek, and added gently, "I don't want you to have pain which can be avoided."

He opened the door, nodded at his wife, crooked a finger at the next patients, and the sisters rose, twittering. A small boy and his mother, who had come in after Lucy went into the office, were waiting, and the mother was saying, "Stop biting your nails!"

Lucy went over to speak to Winnie. "I'm thinking of changing doctors," she announced.

"Don't put Pete down," Winnie advised, smiling.

"Honestly, I could strangle him."

"There are times when I could. I'll call you in an hour or so about the arrangements. Everything's set. I just want to be sure of your room."

"Ulcers," said Lucy with annoyance.

"Not plural, I think; and only pre."

"He told you?"

"Pete doesn't tell me anything unless he has to—in this case with the arrangements to be made and getting hold of Doctor Stevens—"

"Bill Stevens? That child—whatever for?"

"He's a specialist, Lucy. Pete wants him, as a consultant."

"Your husband," Lucy remarked, "is a worrier. He should have ulcers."

"Oh, he did," Winnie told her. "Shortly after we were married."

Lucy said, as the door opened and three more patients came in, "Well, thanks, I'll hear from you."

"Of course, and at the same time we'll make that dinner date . . . for after you're out of the hospital."

"You'll eat," Lucy predicted. "I'll toy with baby food."

"It won't be that bad," Winnie said.

Lucy walked back to the library. If there had to be something wrong with her, why couldn't it be interesting? She remembered Sam saying often, "How you dote on the dramatic."

All right, Sam . . . tests, diet, and longer naps. If Pete was right, and he probably was . . . Very boring, she thought: Perhaps for ten or fifteen years.

What could she do with them?

Reba, when she got over the shock of the hospital bit, would insist on talking with Pete. He'd anticipated that. After which she would supervise everything, diet, rest periods. Lucy thought: I might persuade her in the circumstances to go to Florida with me.

She halted a moment, and then walked on, thinking, in mild astonishment: But I don't really want to return to Florida. It bores me too.

I could stay home, she thought, and if Viki needs me, I'll be here. Maybe Jenny would come now and then. Perhaps I'll write Edward at his Club; perhaps he'd come up, and we could talk. I've always been able to talk with him. Not that seeing Viki or talking to Edward would solve anything. I've never solved anything in my life, she reminded herself. Not really, but just being around might give Viki an anchor . . . or even Cynthia, after a while.

She felt relieved, also singularly foolish . . . all the things she'd imagined . . . cancer had been uppermost in her mind. Pete could be wrong, of course, but she doubted it. Doctor Stevens—she knew his parents—was young, attractive, and, she supposed, extremely competent. He was also un-married. Viki might like him, she decided, and then laughed at herself.

She reached the Library and got into the car. Reba would be anxious. Maybe she'd already called Pete.

Reba, thought Lucy, is an old woman. So am I. Perhaps I can induce her to board a plane and go with me to see Rhoda. She would, if only to see that I eat the right things.

Lucy had promised herself ten years ago that she'd never set foot on Spanish soil again. If she saw Rhoda, Rhoda would have to come to her.

We'll see, she thought.

It was still June, coasting into July. Life was all around her, growing, maturing, dying, returning. . . .

The little pain pinched her tentatively. She spoke to it again. She said, "Don't be silly; you're licked."

Driving up to the house, she was conscious of every-thing with a heightened awareness: flowers, birds, trees, the sky, the clouds, the house itself . . . and also of a slight elusive fragrance in the car. Stopping at her own door, she tried to identify it.

Yellow Iris.

"Don't be fanciful," she admonished herself, got out of the car, and saw Reba open the front door. Smiling, she went to meet her.